Also by Natasha Frazier

The Life Your Spirit Craves

Not Without You

*Love,
Lies &
Consequences*

CHAPTER 1

∞

Raegan stood at the entrance to the sanctuary on the arm of her father. The double doors remained closed as they waited to hear the wedding processional, signaling it was time for them to enter. She was so nervous that the bouquet of roses and lilies was starting to slide around in her hands.

She was about to make one of the biggest commitments in her life. Marriage. She believed in *till death do us part* and had dreamed of this day since high school, but right now she wondered if she was making the right choice by marrying Damian.

All had been well in her mind until her weekend getaway with her girls last month. They traveled to Miami as sort of a last hoorah for Raegan before she tied the knot.

The weekend was perfect at first. They entertained themselves with spa appointments, fine dining, sightseeing, shopping, and time on the beaches.

During her last night in town, they dined at Rusty Pelican, one of Miami's waterfront restaurants that offers a stunning view of the skyline. She must have chosen the perfect seat because she had a great view of everything from the entrance of the restaurant to the people walking along the beach and the gorgeous skyline. Although it was nearing dusk and she had a few sips of wine, she was very clear on who she saw in that moment. Caleb. She could identify him anywhere. He was strolling along the beach with a few friends, people she did not recognize.

She thought her father would be giving her hand to Caleb, but Caleb messed that up some time ago. But there he was again. A slight smile formed on her face when she thought about their time together back in college. That smile quickly turned into a frown when she remembered how and why things ended between them. She didn't mention seeing him to her friends. He didn't notice her and neither of her friends noticed him, but her facial expressions changed so quickly that her friends expressed concern. "Oh, it's just some food that caught between my teeth," she told them with a wince and a small laugh.

Now here she was, on the arm of her father walking down the aisle to join in holy matrimony with Damian Charles. The wedding processional played and started to sound more blurry by the moment. She could see the goofy smile plastered across Damian's face as his legs visibly shook. The closer she got to the altar, the more she realized that something wasn't right.

She took slow, deep breaths, reminding herself that this was just a case of cold feet and that she could do this. This was her moment. She recalled the day he proposed. He took her to the movies. They went at midday on a Saturday afternoon and she thought it strange that they were the only two people in the theater. As the previews began rolling, she gasped. Pictures of the two of them played across the screen until finally the last screen displayed a diamond ring with the words, "Will You Marry Me?"

Without much hesitation, she said *yes*. There were no butterflies like she thought there would be; her heart was not fluttering with excitement. They had been dating for about a year. He asked and she accepted. To rethink all of this now was bad timing, but the closer she got to the altar, the more she wanted to bolt out of the door.

She caught glimpses of the flashing cameras and smiling faces of family and friends until the next thing she realized the pastor was asking who was giving her away. Her mom stood along with her dad and in unison, they said, "We do." Her father kissed her forehead and placed her hand inside of Damian's. He whispered into Damian's ear, "Take care of my baby girl."

As she walked hand in hand with Damian toward the pastor, she began to tremble even more. She turned and placed the bouquet in her maid of honor's hand. She stepped closer to Damian and placed both hands in his. As the ceremony continued around her, she stared blindly into her husband-to-be's eyes. She couldn't see him, though. All she could see were thoughts of Caleb and *what-ifs*. This probably wouldn't have happened had she not seen him last month. However, it was happening, and she knew that it wouldn't be fair to Damian to spend the rest of her life with him wondering how things would have turned out with another man.

She thought of how things started and the current state of their relationship. They were moving too fast. Pre-marital sex and living together; it was as if they were already married. *The relationship is already doomed,* she thought. *We can't do this,* she reasoned with herself. Her heart was beating double time now.

"Raegan, do you take Damian to be your lawfully wedded husband?" Pastor asked. He must have asked more than once because she felt Damian's gentle tug on her hand, bringing her back into the present.

"I…I…I do…I do not. I'm so sorry Damian; I can't do this," Raegan said as she slipped her fingers out of his, grabbed her dress so that she wouldn't trip, and ran back down the aisle. She rushed inside the bride's holding room, locked the door, and quickly peeled off her dress in tears and relief, thinking that she may have avoided one of the biggest mistakes of her life.

Seconds after she stepped out of the wedding gown, Damian's mother and sister were banging on the door.

"Raegan! What are you thinking? You better get your behind back down that aisle and marry my brother!" his sister screamed through the door.

"Hush girl!" Raegan heard Damian's mother say. "What is going on with you Raegan? Your parents and I spent a great deal of money making this wedding happen for y'all. Come out of there, now!" she demanded.

"Please, just let me be," she stated faintly, leaning against the door.

Raegan felt the knob jiggling in her back. She stepped away when she realized that a key was being inserted. Her heart sank to the floor. She didn't think of others having the key when she locked the door. To Raegan's relief, her mother entered the room, pushing Damian's mom and sister out of the way. "Let me talk to my baby," she said. She gently closed the door behind her, drowning out some of the sound of Damian's mother spewing much angrier words than before.

"What happened out there, dear?" her mother asked in a quiet, non-judgmental tone.

Raegan didn't answer. She just stared back at her mother in silence. She wasn't quite sure why she allowed things to get this far, but she was certain it shouldn't go any further and this was the right thing to do.

Glancing at the dress on the floor, her mother said, "I take it you're not planning to go back out there?"

"I can't Momma. I feel like a terrible person for leading Damian on this way. I should have said *no* to his proposal." She paused, giving her mother a moment to speak, but when her mother said nothing Raegan continued. "This just feels wrong. It's almost as if we're married now because we're living as if we're married. I want a better relationship with the man I'm going to marry. I need sparks and lights in my eyes. Besides, I want a marriage that is blessed by God. I want to do things right. No shacking and no sex until marriage," Raegan said.

"It's your life, Raegan, and I can't tell you what to do. However, you can't leave Damian like this. You're going to have to be a woman and tell him that you're not going to marry him. If you want a right relationship with God and the man you are to marry, make sure you settle this now," her mother advised.

"But how am I supposed to go back out there? I don't even know what to say." Raegan chewed on her bottom lip as she paced the floor. "How can I even face him right now? Especially with his mother and sister outside of that door probably wanting to kill me."

"Raegan," her mother said in a tone that caused her to stop pacing, "I did not raise you to act like this. You're going to have to get it together. Is there something you're not telling me?" Her mother walked over and lifted Raegan's chin so that she could see Raegan's eyes when she answered.

"What do you mean Momma?" Raegan whined a little. "The truth is that this isn't going to work. Not now, not ever. I don't love him the way he loves me and I think I deserve to be truly happy," Raegan said, thinking of the only person she had been truly happy with before things went wrong.

Raegan spoke without blinking. Her mother knew that there was something Raegan wasn't telling her but she would find out soon enough. She advised Raegan again to talk with Damian. Now his voice was the only voice outside of the door calling her name, asking for answers. She could tell he was hurting by the sound of his voice.

The door banging and screams from his mother and sister had ceased. After she felt confident enough, she opened the door to allow Damian to enter. He had taken his jacket off, loosened his tie and unbuttoned the first few buttons of his shirt. Her heart broke for him but she cared enough for him not to spend the rest of her life lying to him and wishing he was someone else. He walked past her and stood silently waiting for answers. Her eyes pleaded with her mother for help but instead, her mother shot her a look that said *you're on your own.* She left them alone to talk and sent the guests to the reception to enjoy the food.

CHAPTER 2

∞

Precisely two years had passed since Raegan left Damian standing at the altar, confused and heartbroken. It was likely one of the worst things that happened to him but one of the best things she could have done for herself. Whether or not he realized it then, she saved him a lifetime of heartache because she was still in love with someone else. She knew she would never be able to love him and treat him with the respect he deserved without some sort of resentment. She didn't want to spend her days dreaming of another man. She would be devastated if she found out that her husband's heart belonged to someone else the way hers did.

After the failed nuptials, Raegan moved out of the place she shared with Damian and stayed with Tammy for a while before purchasing her own home. Since then, Raegan had taken the time to grow spiritually and focus on her professional career. She was quickly climbing the corporate ladder and was proud of her accomplishments, but she would definitely be lying to herself if she said that she didn't want to be married; she just didn't want to marry the wrong guy.

Raegan's thoughts were interrupted by the honking of the car horn behind her. The signal light had turned green and she hadn't even noticed.

Soon she arrived at her destination. Slipping her two-door coupe into park, she stepped out to see two of her friends waiting for her outside of Pappadeaux for dinner.

"Hey Rae!" both Tammy and Michelle said in unison.

"Hey ladies!" she said, walking into their embraces. "You both look gorgeous!"

"We all do," said Tammy with a giggle.

The restaurant was crowded with young professionals who were ready to celebrate the weekend. They were escorted to a booth near the rear of the restaurant, for which they were all grateful because they wanted to chat and enjoy the scenery.

When they were seated, Michelle turned to Raegan. "Rae, we know that today would have been your two-year anniversary to Damian. How are you holding up?"

"I'm actually doing pretty well. Have you all heard anything about him? How is he?" Raegan wrinkled her nose, her tone almost a whisper.

"He's fine, I guess, but we're concerned about you," Tammy said.

"Well, that's good. You all know that work is keeping me busy. I'm preparing for my next promotion," Raegan said proudly. While speaking, she noticed a handsome man walking toward their table. He stopped right beside Raegan and asked, "Is there anything that I can do for you?"

"Are you our waiter?" She wondered because they had yet to receive any service, not even glasses of water.

"I can be whoever you want me to be," he said, smiling at her.

"I take it you're not going to be serving us then?" she said and smiled back. "If you can find our waiter, that would be great," Raegan said and turned her attention back toward her friends as he walked away.

Michelle gasped. "Rae, you do know that he was flirting with you, right? Aren't you waiting for Mr. Right? Missy, *that* could have been him." Michelle has been on the quest for Mr. Right over the last several years. She was now on her third engagement.

"I doubt it. No butterflies," Raegan stated as she dismissed the idea.

Shaking her head, Tammy said, "You turn down everybody. It's almost as if you're waiting on…"

"Waiting on what?" Raegan quickly interrupted, almost daring her to say his name.

"Caleb," Michelle and Tammy both blurted his name as if they had been rehearsing it all evening. Michelle folded her arms and began to lecture Raegan on giving love a chance and not worrying about Caleb, especially since she claimed that she didn't want to be with him. Their relationship had ended horribly years ago. Raegan hadn't spoken to him since they ended things back in college. However, seeing him shortly before her wedding sparked something inside of her. She just didn't know exactly what.

After they finally received service and had dinner, the friends parted ways.

"Don't forget about my Labor Day party tomorrow," Tammy said as they left the restaurant. Tammy had invited quite a few people from her alma mater's alumni chapter and was hoping that Raegan would meet someone there. She knew that her friend desired love and hoped that tomorrow could be a great start.

***

"Why aren't you married?" Rico asked Raegan. Raegan caught Rico's eye during a game of Taboo at Tammy's Labor Day party. He waited patiently for the opportunity to talk with her; when he finally got the chance, he wanted to know more about her relationship status. He admired her beauty, and when he noticed she wasn't wearing a wedding band, he promised himself that he would not leave Tammy's house without talking to Raegan.

"Am I supposed to be?" She didn't have an attitude, but her tone depicted that it wasn't really any of his business either. She gave him a once-over. He wasn't the most handsome man that she had met but he was kept. His receding hairline gave her the impression that he was at least thirty years old, and at that age, she figured, most men started looking for a woman to marry.

"Well you're beautiful and intelligent." He was trying to charm her in order to get her to open up. Rico was used to women being receptive to his slick words, but they didn't fool Raegan one bit.

"Is that all it takes to qualify to be a wife?" Raegan asked with raised eyebrows.

"Well no, but I'm sitting here talking to you and I haven't found a flaw yet. What are your flaws?" Rico questioned as he made himself comfortable on the couch next to Raegan.

"Why are you looking for them? Why does it matter to you?" At this point, she was wondering why on earth she was even sitting there entertaining him. She glanced around the room quickly to find any sign of Tammy. Tammy wasn't anywhere to be found.

"I just want to know why a woman as beautiful as you are is still single."

This is what happens when you go to parties and you only know the host, she thought. Her friend Tammy had purchased her home a couple of years ago and this Labor Day barbeque was her first party welcoming friends and family to her new place. The house was really nice, located in a cul-de-sac in a gorgeous master planned community. Tammy's house was one story with three bedrooms, a game room, two and a half baths, and a two car garage.

Michelle stopped by the party but Raegan could not spot her either. Tammy and Raegan attended different schools and had different professional circles. She met Tammy at a networking event about a year ago. Most of the attendees were people who went to Tammy's alma mater, and Raegan was not a social butterfly.

During Taboo, while Raegan was giving clues to her team Rico would blurt out things just so that she would notice him. He loved attention. She could tell by his T-shirt that said *Every Woman's Dream.* Now he was sitting next to her asking her hundreds of questions about herself.

Answering Rico's question, Raegan said, "If you must know, the men that I've crossed paths with and have an interest in usually can't measure up to the standards that I set or accept my lifestyle."

"What lifestyle is that?" Rico asked, becoming even more intrigued.

"Man, you're nosey!" Raegan knew that he was trying to feel her out but thought that since her answer was personal, he was being rather personal.

"You left yourself wide open for that question. Tell me."

Raegan tossed her curls away from her face and adjusted her tube top before speaking. It was obvious that Rico was giving too much attention to other parts of her body. "I'm celibate. Guys say they can handle that but they really can't and I completely understand. It's a choice. We choose what we want and if one should choose to be sexually active, then one may as well choose someone who is making the same kind of choice, right?"

"I understand that. My mother is a pastor so I try not to do anything that will reflect badly on her."

"Oh okay," Raegan said, eyeing him carefully. Raegan wondered at this point if his love was greater for his mother or for God.

"I'm serious. I'm not giving myself to anyone else until I'm in a serious relationship. I have met so many women who only want the physical part of me and don't want to know the real me," Rico said in an attempt to empathize with her.

Unable to control her chuckle, she asked, "Are you serious?" Now that was a new pick-up line.

"Yes, it is true. There have been times when I've been sick and couldn't get anyone to check on me, but if I wanted to have sex, she would be right there," Rico explained.

Raegan thought that this sounded pretty weird. He seemed to be arrogant and self-centered. Based on her quick assessment of him, he didn't have a reason to be arrogant. She decided that she would definitely get out of the house before he could ask for her number.

"Well perhaps you're just dealing with the wrong kind of women," Raegan said as she stood up to find Tammy.

"Maybe I am. Maybe I am," Rico said with a smirk on his face and a light in his eyes that told Raegan that she hadn't heard the last from him.

CHAPTER 3

∞

I finally found you. Hello Ms. Lady. We met at a barbeque about a month ago. How are you? I know this is forward but here is my number. I would love to hear from you. Rico "Interesting," Raegan said as she read the private Facebook message. Raegan definitely wasn't going to call but decided that she would accept his friend request.

A month had passed since Tammy's Labor Day party. Raegan didn't give Rico her number before she left but she had a feeling that she would somehow hear from him again. Until today, Raegan had not heard a peep from Rico; in fact, she had forgotten the interaction.

Just then Raegan's cell phone started ringing.

"Hey Rae!" It was Tammy. Tammy was always so bubbly and energetic, wearing a smile on her face like sunshine all the time. Although Tammy was very sweet, she was also honest, lacking any sort of filter. One never had to guess what she was thinking because she would certainly say what was on her mind.

"Tammy, what's up? I was just about to give you a call. Guess who sent me a friend request on Facebook?"

"I don't know. Tell me"

"Guess? I met him at the gathering you had at your place last month."

"Rico?" Tammy questioned. She was a bit skeptical about this interaction.

"Yes ma'am. That's him. We had a long conversation at your party, remember?"

"I remember all right. I thought you weren't interested in him. A classmate told me several times to come rescue you because he was bothering you. Was he?"

"No, he was just being arrogant. He mentioned some stuff about his promiscuous ways in undergrad and how he's changed so much...blah, blah, blah. He's looking for his 'queen,' he says. That had nothing to do with me, but for some reason he felt the need to share that with me."

Tammy didn't know a lot about him; he was only invited to the party because the invitation went to the entire alumni chapter. She felt the need to warn Raegan. "Please be careful."

"No worries."

"All right girl. I'm off to a happy hour. I was calling you to see if you wanted to hang out tonight," Tammy said.

"I'm going to pass. I'm a little tired. I'll catch up with you over the weekend," Raegan declined the invitation.

After arriving home, Raegan slid into her lounge clothes to catch up on her DVR as planned, along with her favorite glass of wine. After being engrossed in the television for a few hours, she checked her messages to find that she had received another Facebook message from Rico. *"Hello Ms. Lady. It was really great to meet you and I'd like to chat with you sometime. May I call you? Inbox me your number."*

Boredom and a little bit of curiosity got the best of her, so she sent him her number. Immediately, she received a text message from him asking about her day. After two hours of texting, she thought that maybe her first impression of him may not have been completely accurate. He was more interesting than she remembered.

"Will you go out with me?" Raegan could not believe what she was reading. *He obviously has me mixed up with someone else if he thinks that I am going to accept an invitation to go out with him via text message,* she thought.

Raegan responded to his text. "I do not go out with guys who ask me out through text message."

"Give me a few minutes," responded Rico.

About five minutes passed and the lovely song of Mozart began to play through her Blackberry. It was Rico.

"Hello," Raegan said after she allowed the phone to ring for a few seconds.

"Hey Gorgeous! Your voice is even sweeter than I remember," Rico said.

"So you say…"

"Yeah…that's right. Is there a chance that I can hear that beautiful voice in person again soon?"

"I don't know…" Raegan said. If he wanted her to go out with him, he was going to have to ask her directly. She wasn't going to play his game.

"You have to know that I haven't been able to stop thinking about you since we met. I would like to take you out to see a movie, go to the museum, picnic, or whatever you like. It really doesn't matter; I just want to spend some time in your presence." Rico said. "Are you free next weekend?"

There was a new movie coming out that she wanted to see. "Hmmm…Seeing a movie sounds good, but only if I get to pick the movie. We can meet at Edward Cinema in Greenway Plaza at 7:30 p.m. next Saturday. Sound good?" Raegan set the date.

"As long as I get to see your pretty face," Rico agreed to the details.

"Okay, I have to go, so I will see you next weekend," Raegan said as she ended the call.

***

Raegan met Rico at the movie theater promptly at 7:30 p.m. as agreed. She wore a gold sequin tank top, blue jeans and a pair of pumps. Her hair was curly as usual, but today it was glossy because she visited the beauty shop earlier that morning.

"Wow, you look amazing!" Rico exclaimed as soon as Raegan was within earshot. He had arrived early and stood in front of the theater waiting for her to arrive. He was glad that he had done so because it was a pleasure to see her walking toward him in all of her beauty. He hadn't thought that he had even the smallest chance with her after their initial meeting at Tammy's party but decided to take a shot anyway. He was thankful for Facebook.

"Thank you. Are you ready for the movie? I am pretty sure that Channing Tatum is going to give us another amazing performance," Raegan said excited to watch her favorite actor.

"Well, let's see," he said, extending his arm toward the door. He had already purchased the tickets. Rico didn't care which movie they went to see, he just wanted to spend that time with her.

Raegan didn't mind movie dates because she didn't have to talk. It wasn't personal. All she had to do was sit there and watch the movie. Those types of dates usually turned out well.

He purchased drinks, candy and popcorn before they found seats in the theater. They had arrived in just the right amount of time. The theater began filling up pretty quickly.

She noticed that he was polite during the movie. He didn't attempt to put his arm around her or make any moves. Every now and again, he would comment about different scenes. After the movie ended, he suggested that they grab dessert so that they could spend some time talking and getting to know each other.

"Where would you like to go?" he asked her.

"There's an ice cream shop right down the street. We can go there."

Rico didn't care much for ice cream but he wanted to spend more time admiring her beauty and getting to know her more. He was intrigued by Raegan. He had never met another woman like her.

Since they hadn't driven to the theater together, they each took their own car to the ice cream shop. Once inside, he found them a table and they waited for the waitress to take their order.

They discussed their favorite parts of the movie before Rico switched the subject. "So, tell me, what do you do?"

"I work downtown for a Fortune 500 company in HR. I've been there about six years now. When I first started, I worked with employees who filed sexual harassment complaints. I've since moved away from that and I work in recruitment, which is much more fun," she said.

"That sounds interesting. I'm sure you've heard a lot of stories."

"I have. The first assignment was too personal for me. I needed something lighter. Now, I get to help students and some people who are mid-career find the perfect place within our company. I enjoy that."

"I see. Your face lights up when you talk about it."

"What about you? What do you do?" she asked, putting a spoonful of ice cream in her mouth. The waitress had just returned with their desserts and she didn't waste any time digging into hers.

"I work in sales. I sell luxury vehicles."

"Now, that's interesting. How did you get into that?" she asked.

"It's actually a career change. I used to be in social work but I didn't like it. I found it draining, plus it didn't pay very well. I have a friend who works at the dealership who suggested that I give it a shot. I've been there about six months now," said Rico.

They continued to talk about work, church involvement and their favorite things over ice cream until near closing of the shop.

"This was fun," said Raegan as she finished her ice cream. "But I need to get home and get ready for morning worship service. I'm not volunteering tomorrow so I need to get there in enough time to find a seat."

"I had a great time. Thank you for spending some time with me tonight. I hope that we can do this again soon," Rico said, standing and helping her out of her seat. He walked her to her car, helped her inside and made sure that she was safely out of the parking lot before leaving. He wanted to see more of her and he knew just how to make that happen –church!

As Raegan rode home, she reflected on her time with Rico. Surprisingly, she enjoyed herself. The more she thought about her date, the more her thoughts traveled back to when she first met Rico and she revealed that she was celibate. She thought that would be enough to run him off but she was wrong.

She was reminded of a recent conversation with a male friend who suggested that she would never get married if she remained celibate because she was never going to meet a guy who would feel the same way about sex. She wasn't sure of what Rico's stance was on the issue, but figured that he may not have a problem with it since he looked her up and asked her out after she told him that there wouldn't be any sex.

Her celibacy hadn't been an issue in the past two years because she hadn't seriously dated anyone. *The true test of my commitment will come when I am actually tested, but it's nothing I can't handle,* she thought.

CHAPTER 4

∞

Rico decided that he would surprise Raegan and visit her church on Sunday. He knew that her faith was a big part of her life and he wanted to show her that he was interested in getting to know her on all levels. He saw by the huge grin on her face when she made eye contact with him that his efforts were appreciated.

Raegan was surprised to see Rico standing off to the side of the sanctuary entrance waiting for her when she entered the building. He greeted her with a kiss to the back of her hand before they walked into the sanctuary.

As always Raegan enjoyed the service. Rico expressed that he liked the pastor's sermon, although he spent a great deal of time watching her. After the benediction, Rico whispered into her ear that he had to leave. She was hoping they would be able to have brunch since he had taken the time out to visit her there.

He told her that he had something to take care of at home, although he wasn't specific about it. Getting away to go to church was the easy part; it would have been strenuous for him to come up with reasons as to why he was gone for several hours. He enjoyed spending time with Raegan, so brunch with her could have easily turned into a two-hour event.

After church, Raegan called her best friend and sorority sister, Kensi. Not only was Kensi her best friend, but Kensi had also come to be her accountability partner. Kensi helped Raegan focus on her goals when it came to celibacy. In fact, they made a celibacy pact. Neither of them would have sex again before marriage.

"Raegan! What's going on? I haven't heard from you all weekend missy! What's up with that?" Kensi exclaimed jokingly. Even though they were on the phone, Raegan knew that Kensi was wagging her finger around.

"Kens Kens Kens! How are you sis?" she sang in a cheery voice. She was very upbeat that afternoon. After going to church earlier that morning she felt empowered again. She began to share her notes from the sermon with Kensi. "Pastor's sermon topic today was 'This is only a test.' It was pretty good too. He discussed how our responses should be when God tests us. He explained that God often tests us at the place of our affection. When we love the blessings of God more than God, often He will test us. Testing is the only way to prove what we say we believe. He also mentioned that God tests us because He is trying to promote us. We can't have great blessings and weak tests. Our faith has to be equivalent to the blessings we are about to receive."

"Oh, sounds like you took some good notes there buddy," Kensi said as she scribbled down a few of the points to review later.

"Of course I did. I always do." Raegan was very proud of herself for taking notes and keeping up with her Bible studying.

"Yes, the sermon was really good and it really touched my spirit. I am more encouraged than I was yesterday in my daily walk with God," Raegan continued.

"I am happy to hear that. So what else is going on? That is just where you were today. I haven't heard from you all weekend," Kensi said as a matter of fact.

"Well…I actually went out on a date last night," Raegan said, leaving Kensi to probe for details.

"Oh really! Which guy? Spill the details." Kensi loved to tease Raegan because it seemed like she dated a different guy every month, discarding them as if they were old newspapers.

"That's funny. What do you mean which guy?"

"Hey, it's not my fault you have so many to choose from."

"That is definitely not true!" Raegan never thought this, but all of her friends believed that she had a plethora of guys to choose from. She believed her pickings were very slim. "I'm not sure if I told you about him or not. He is the pushy guy I met at Tammy's Labor Day gathering. Did I tell you about that?"

"Nope. Doesn't ring a bell," Kensi said as if to hurry Raegan along with the more important details of her date.

Raegan gave her a quick recap of the first time they met and then continued with details regarding her date.

"We met at the movie theater. When I first walked up to meet him, he says, 'You look amazing.'"

"He is either a sweetie or a master at the game," Kensi interjected.

"That is true but it was cute nonetheless." Raegan continued, "We went to see the new Channing Tatum movie. I thought it was pretty good and had an unexpected end. I'm not sure if he enjoyed it all that much even though he said he did. Afterwards we went to grab dessert from an ice cream shop."

As Raegan chatted on about her date, Kensi noticed that she wasn't providing any of Rico's basic information, forcing Kensi to probe even more.

"Raegan, you're killing me here! Give me the real deets! What does homeboy do? How old is he? Does he love the Lord? Where does he go to church? Where is he from? Did he go to school? You know! All of the basic background questions," Kensi said dramatically.

"Sorry," Raegan laughed off Kensi's dramatic outburst. "You're funny. I like the detective in you, though. I guess I forgot to mention that he came to my church this morning."

Interrupting her, Kensi said, "Wait, what? Now that is interesting. I guess that answers my questions about his love for the Lord. Or maybe he was just trying to get next to you."

"Maybe…" Raegan said as she thought about Kensi's assessment of him. She continued, "He is 31 and he's a new car salesman. He is from a very small town in Alabama that you nor I have ever heard of and probably never will. Google him."

"Don't worry, I'm way ahead of you. I started after you gave me his name. I haven't found anything interesting yet though, only his Twitter and Facebook page appeared in the search results. No, wait! Here's the link to an article about him in Social Services from his previous job," Kensi noted. She skipped around other articles that appeared in the search results that seemed to be irrelevant.

"I saw that already. Keep looking and let me know if you find anything," Raegan instructed.

"So back to this date, what were his conversational skills like?" Kensi closed her laptop; she was interested in hearing this story because Raegan never really went into much detail about anyone, so she figured that she must really like this guy.

"He talked quite a bit about his family. He gets points because it appears that he really adores his mother. He actually takes care of her. I'm not sure whether that's a good or bad thing though. He talked about his ambitions and how he isn't interested in playing games because he's looking for his wife." Raegan wasn't necessarily impressed by the "looking for his wife" statement. That is what most guys told her because they believed that she was "wife-material." Guys figured that would be the only way to keep her attention at least for a little while.

"He sounds like a good catch so far. Just remember to take your time and if in any way he doesn't align with what you're trying to do for yourself, then don't hesitate to leave him alone," Kensi cautioned Raegan.

Kensi usually didn't have to give this kind of advice to Raegan, but she could sense that something was different about the way she felt with this guy as opposed to others. Raegan was all giddy, which was a trait no one had used to describe her since she dated Caleb. Kensi figured there had to be something to this guy.

"So what exactly have you been up to this weekend, Kensi? We've talked enough about me dear."

"Nothing much. I've just been sitting here watching some of the shows that I taped on my DVR." As Kensi talked on the phone to Raegan, she was busy doing work as well. Kensi was a successful journalist. She really enjoyed her work, so she spent her time working even when she wasn't at work. Whenever she was home, she was working or doing something that would enhance her career in some sort of way. She didn't describe herself as a "workaholic"; she simply took pleasure in her work.

"Okay. How are things in the Big Apple? When are you coming down south for a visit? You know I just bought a house, so you're definitely due for a visit!"

"Yes! I have a training scheduled there soon, so I will keep you posted," Kensi informed Raegan.

Kensi was satisfied that she didn't find anything negative about Rico via her Google search; they finished their chat and said their good-byes. When the call ended, Raegan continued to reflect on her first date with Rico, trying to figure out what was it about him that made her giddy. She didn't feel the same amount of excitement as she once felt with Caleb, but it was the most enthusiasm she had felt for a guy in quite a while.

CHAPTER 5

∞

Rico called Raegan on the way to work Wednesday morning, just a few days after their first date. He asked her out for lunch. Her schedule was very busy during the end of the calendar year, and lunch was just about the only time she had for anything else other than work during the weekdays, so she agreed. *You have to eat anyway* is how he convinced her to go out with him midday.

They both worked downtown in the business district, which made it quite convenient for them to connect and have lunch. A variety of shops, businesses, and restaurants in the area could meet just about every need one could possibly have. They decided upon a Cajun cafeteria-style restaurant to eliminate wait time and allow them to get back to work in an hour.

While waiting in line, Rico bragged about himself, all the while calling himself a humble person. This always made her chuckle to herself, because she believed that those who were humble in spirit didn't have to *say* they were humble; it would surely show in the way they lived. They discussed what a typical day was like for them during and after work. Rico explained that he lived a pretty boring life. After work, he generally watched sports and reality television or spent time surfing the internet.

"No hobbies?" she asked him with a sarcastic smile. Considering the things he told her before about having a passion for helping people, she thought he would be volunteering his time, especially since he got off work while it was still daylight. He didn't really answer her question. He just stood there with a smirk on his face, hands in his pockets, rocking back and forth on his heels, talking about how he was a servant at heart.

Raegan tossed her curls away from her face and began to look at the menu to decide what she would eat.

"So what will it be for you, young lady?" the server asked.

"I'll take the chicken and sausage gumbo with extra rice," she said with a bright smile. She often came there with her colleagues, especially on Thursdays and Fridays when they served the seafood gumbo. They all loved it and made special trips down almost every week to grab some for lunch.

"What will it be for you, chief?" the server asked Rico.

"I'll have the baked chicken breast with cornbread and macaroni and cheese."

Raegan found them a table. It was usually difficult around lunchtime, but she managed to find one so that they wouldn't have to stand and wait with the trays in their hands until a table became available. She waited for him before she began her meal. She bowed her head and silently asked God to bless her food but her prayer was interrupted when she felt Rico's hands grab hers. She glanced up and he smiled at her. She was quite surprised by his actions and just followed his lead. He asked God to bless their food and thanked Him for bringing the two of them together. She was so pleased and taken aback by Rico's act of boldness that she was now speechless. Raegan had dated quite a few guys and never had any of them done such a thing since Caleb.

After such an audacious move, she was convinced that she had judged him too quickly and maybe he was a man after God's own heart and quite possibly the man for her. *A man who took initiative to pray for the two of us deserved a chance*, she thought. Throughout lunch, her thoughts began to swirl and imagine what life would be like with him. Just as she was daydreaming about happily ever after, she was jolted back to reality by Rico singing her name. "Rayyyyyygan."

"Oh, I'm sorry. Repeat your question," she said, slightly embarrassed because she had no idea what he was chiming on about.

"I was asking how things are going for you with your new project in preparation for your next promotion."

"It's going well. There are a lot of working parts but I'm up to the challenge," she chatted on about her new project. "As a matter of fact, I really need to get back to work to complete a presentation that I have later this week. I appreciate lunch," Raegan said as she checked the time on her watch and gathered her purse.

"Would you like to take a brownie to go?" asked Rico.

"No, but I will definitely take a piece of German chocolate cake!" Raegan said as she grabbed the goodie.

Before she could say good-bye and walk away, Rico pulled her into a quick embrace. She could feel the warmth of his breath on her forehead.

"You'll be seeing a lot more of me, woman," Rico said after hugging her.

"I think I may be looking forward to it," she smiled as she stepped out of his arms and turned to walk back to her building.

CHAPTER 6

∞

The sage linen curtains in Raegan's room hardly kept the sunlight from shining through her windows in the mornings. Most of the time, if her alarm clock didn't frustrate her enough to get her out of bed, the beautiful rays of sunshine did the trick, as was the case this morning. Raegan rolled out of bed to get her day started. She read her devotional lesson for the morning, which led her to Scriptures on patience. She really needed that particular guidance because patience was one of the many things she struggled with.

As she sat propped up in her bed studying, her phone sang, "You've Got Mail!" She leaned over to put her phone on silent mode so that she could fully focus on what God was trying to say to her before she started her day. She continued to study and pray, asking God for patience. She knew she needed to be careful about what she asked for because God would certainly grant her request by allowing her to go through situations that would help her become more patient. She wasn't quite sure if she was ready for that but, she was all about becoming a better person.

After finishing her devotional and morning routine of getting ready for work, she took a look at her phone to see who sent her a message so early in the morning. The e-mail was from Rico, so she decided to wait until she arrived at work to read it. A few weeks had passed since their movie outing, and communication between the two of them was starting to pick up.

As she walked out of the elevator bank through the double glass doors of her company's office space, she saw two of her colleagues going to get coffee before their weekly staff meeting at 9:30 a.m. She was happy to be inside, away from Houston's unforgiving humidity. As she continued to walk to her office, she admired the office décor, although most people would probably consider it a little old-fashioned and outdated. The walls were plain but the wall art was inspirational. A statue by the front entrance intrigued her, but she had no idea what it actually was. It was close to bronze in color and the bottom of it was shaped like a baby's bottom, while the top of it was some unknown shape. Regardless of that, she has always admired the figure.

Once inside of her office, she immediately remembered the unread e-mail from Rico so she checked her personal e-mail account to read the message on her cell phone. As she read it, her face lit up. She thought to herself, *"This guy doesn't let up easy. He is working really hard."* The e-mail read:

Good morning,

This letter comes to share my thoughts concerning you and our future together. In recent months, I have been through many associations with women who never had my attention or interest from day one; they were merely someone to cure my boredom.

The qualities and traits that I looked for in a woman, I did not see in them and I honestly began to think I had set my standards too high, and the woman created for me did not exist. I left the dating arena and started to do a self-reflection to ensure that I brought to the table all the traits necessary for a great relationship, and I re-tooled and dropped some un-needed baggage and I present myself as you see me today.

Upon taking one look at you as you walked through the door at Tammy's, as you made your way to the kitchen I was in awe. I took a back seat and watched your actions, how you sat, spoke, interacted, and said to myself, "I know she's off the market." I checked your finger for a sign of marriage, watched your eyes to see if I could read anything. Finally I had the opportunity to speak to you and was absolutely mesmerized!!! I had every intention on asking for your number to communicate with you, but that was not the route that GOD had for us. The true value of a treasure is not found in the treasure itself, but the effort put forth in finding it. I am happy my hard work produced such a beautiful harvest. I wish you could have seen the look on my face when I found you! I know it's corny, but it has not been many moments in my life when I felt such emotion. How could a woman that I barely know anything about, have such an effect on me? And then we finally made contact and I knew at that point you were a keeper! Just know that now that I have you, I have no plans on letting go. Ever!!!

While reading Rico's e-mail, she began to remember the events over the last few weeks. Ever since the first time she agreed to go out with him, he continuously sent her sweet text messages, Facebook messages, and the like. Some of them she even saved to her phone just to read when she thought of him or to share with her friends when describing the type of guy he seemed to be. Most of the messages spoke of her beauty. Others told how he was after her heart and then her hand in marriage. Quite naturally, Raegan was flattered by his words. He said things to her that she had only dreamed of hearing and only heard in romantic films.

Her phone vibrated in her hands, interrupting her thoughts. She received a text from Rico.

"Hey baby, I miss you. Did you get my e-mail?" he asked.

"Yes, I just finished reading it. You'll be receiving a response soon. Let me catch up on some work and I'll reply to you later," she responded to his text.

Good thing they were communicating through text so that he couldn't see the stunned look on her face. She didn't know how she would respond to such a bold e-mail confession, especially since he was expressing such strong feelings so early in their relationship, or whatever they had going on.

Is this real, she silently questioned. She paused for a moment to think about Rico's e-mail. He certainly had a way with words and definitely seemed to really like her. However, she had an uneasy feeling that she attributed to her comparing Rico to Caleb. She compared everyone to him, which is probably why those relationships didn't last.

You've got to let Caleb go if you want to give this thing with Rico a real chance. That relationship has been over for nearly a decade. It is time to let go, she told herself. No matter how she tried to convince herself, she couldn't move on from Caleb until she got closure.

CHAPTER 7

∞

Right around the time Raegan planned to take her morning coffee break, Michelle walked into her office with a troubled look on her face. Raegan didn't know whether to run over and give her a hug, squeezing her tightly until the tears that she knew were about to come started flowing or to just sit there and wait for the words to come pouring out of her mouth.

"Hey, do you want to walk across the street to Starbucks," Michelle asked. A sad smile was plastered across her face that matched the tone of her voice.

Michelle went to grad school with Raegan. They were in many of the same classes and study groups and spent so much time together that their relationship quickly developed into friendship outside of business school. Michelle often depended on Raegan as a sounding board and spiritual counselor, especially since Michelle's relationship with her fiancé wasn't going very well. She had been engaged for almost four months and there was a fight between them every other day. Michelle wasn't sure if she wanted to spend the rest of her life like that. She understood that couples had their ups and downs but to be at each other's throats constantly was a different issue.

Michelle and Jason had several issues that they identified after a couple of premarital counseling sessions, including the marital pressures they put on their relationship by living together. Their relationship had progressed very quickly. The courtship stage was almost nonexistent. After dating for about two weeks, they moved in together and moved full speed ahead. They were in love and took no caution as to how to build a relationship on a solid foundation.

Raegan saw the pained look on Michelle's face and decided it was definitely time for a coffee break. As they walked out of the double glass doors of the office and into the elevator bank, Michelle could no longer contain herself. She lost her composure and her eyes began to well with tears. For a moment, Raegan just stood there waiting for her to speak. As the tone alerting them to the arrival of the elevator resonated in their ears, Raegan grabbed her hand and they entered the empty cabin.

"What's wrong? What happened?" Raegan asked as she squeezed Michelle tightly, giving her a reassuring hug. Before Michelle spoke, Raegan already knew the issue. It was Jason. She was pretty sure that this mess somehow involved him and that the two of them had broken up again.

"I know you're probably tired of me bringing this to you, but I really don't have anyone else to talk to," Michelle said as the tears she tried so hard to hold back were beginning to slowly escape from her brown almond-shaped eyes.

"It's no problem dear. I really don't mind listening to you. What happened?" Raegan asked in a soft, reassuring tone, encouraging Michelle to open up.

"Well we broke up again, and this time just may be the final time. We decided to ride our bikes on the trail near our apartment to give us some time to talk. Too many unsettled emotions are building and I am just not sure how to deal with them just yet," Michelle confided in Raegan.

Michelle explained the conversation to Raegan. Michelle had expressed to Jason that she didn't really want to be around him at that moment. She didn't want to end up in another senseless argument with him. She couldn't hold it any longer; the tears started flowing and they had to stop riding and took a seat on the bench to air out their feelings. She didn't want to cry in front of him because she didn't want to appear irrational, but she just couldn't hold back her frustration anymore. "I know that there will be tough times in marriage, but is it really this hard?" Michelle asked Raegan.

"I've never been married so I don't know," Raegan said truthfully. She thought about her *almost marriage* to Damian and knew that she had to be careful about giving advice in this department.

"You know my history about leaving Damian at the altar. Some people may think that I was wrong for doing that to him and maybe I was wrong for waiting until the last minute to call things off, but I don't regret it. I felt like I was making the wrong decision. For you, you have to search inside your heart and think about why you wanted to marry Jason in the first place. Read what the Scriptures have to say about love and the roles of husbands and wives. Are you willing to be submissive to him and love him in all things? Till death do you part? You don't have to answer this now, but take some time and think about it. This is the rest of your life we're talking about here, so it's best to make a pretty informed decision," Raegan said as they entered the revolving doors of the coffee shop.

Michelle dabbed her eyes as they entered Starbucks. She didn't want to mess up her flawless makeup. It was around 9:45 a.m. so the crowd had dissipated and there was no line and only one customer at the counter. Raegan treated Michelle to a caramel frappuccino the way she herself liked to drink it, a "tall caramel frappuccino with extra caramel and no whip." That drink was sure to brighten anyone's day at least for a little while, especially if one didn't think about the enormous number of calories.

As the barista began to prepare their orders, they walked to the other end of the counter to wait for their drinks.

"So what am I supposed to do?" Michelle asked Raegan, hoping that she would give her answers to the puzzle of her heart.

Thinking for a moment, Raegan questioned, "How exactly does he feel about all of this?"

"Well he wants things to work out. He believes that we can make it work. I'm just not so sure of it. Too many things just keep coming up. I feel like he's keeping too many things from me. I just found out that he has a child. We've been together for nine months now and not one time has he mentioned having a child. So if he's been keeping this from me, what else has he been keeping from me," Michelle paused for a moment in an effort to calm herself.

"I am thinking that the only reason why he mentioned it then is because the minister asked about blended families during our pre-marital counseling session. When we first started dating, we agreed that we would be open with each other. His excuse for not telling me that he has a daughter is that the child's mother would not let him see her. According to him, they live in Michigan and he hasn't seen her since they moved away three years ago. How am I supposed to believe him? And even if it is true, he could have told me the truth in the first place! There's no telling what else he may be hiding."

"So what did you say when you found this out?" Raegan asked, intentionally ignoring Michelle's question.

"Two tall cups of caramel Frappuccino, no whip, extra caramel," the barista called out to them, interrupting their conversation. They picked up their cups and walked out of the building. Although it was about 60 degrees outside, they still enjoyed their cold drinks. Somehow it was very soothing. The perfect treat.

"I was so angry! I started shouting at him during the counseling session. I was embarrassing myself, so I left the session and went home." She chuckled a little at the memory. "Although it wasn't funny, my feelings were hurt. How could he ask me to marry him and not even tell me something as important as this?"

"I'm sorry to hear that," Raegan said.

"Don't be sorry. I really appreciate you listening to me once again. I'm going to get this mess of a life I have straightened out pretty soon. Let's talk about you though. Who is this new mystery man that you've been going on dates with?" Michelle changed the subject. She chose not to discuss Jason's infidelity; she was highly upset about it but didn't want to go into that level of detail at work. Besides, talking some of the issues over with Raegan helped her feel better; and now she would much rather hear about the joy that Raegan was currently experiencing instead of wallowing in her woes.

Raegan smiled remembering her e-mail response to Rico. *From the short time that I have known you, I do see that you possess the characteristics of the man I desire.* And she meant that. She was becoming quite fond of him.

"We can talk about it over lunch later," Raegan said as she gave Michelle one more hug. She could tell that the worry Michelle had when they left the office was now gone or at least had eased.

CHAPTER 8

∞

"I haven't told you today but you are simply amazing," Rico spoke softly and sweetly to Raegan. He was sitting in his office with the door closed. The walls were thin so he did his best to speak in a tone that would allow his phone conversations to remain private.

"And you're the sweetest thing I've ever known," she responded. The lyrics to Lauryn Hill's song came to mind as the words flowed from her lips. A smile spread across her face when she realized it was Rico on the line. He seemed to always call her at work, she realized. The thought hadn't occurred to her until now but it did seem weird that he often called her during work hours; he usually communicated through text message at other times. However, she brushed off the funny feeling.

"Am I really?" Rico asked with a bit of excitement in his voice.

"You are."

"I seriously hope that's what you're thinking about me. Are we still on for dinner at your place tonight?" Rico asked with anticipation. It had been about two weeks since their lunch date. They hadn't been able to connect since. Raegan had been busy with work and Rico always seemed to have something to take care of at home when she was free.

"Yes, of course," Raegan confirmed. Raegan loved to cook and was excited about showing off her cooking skills. "Dinner will be ready around 8:00 p.m. and you don't need to bring anything unless you want dessert. I will not be making any."

"Okay. I will bring cheesecake. Which do you prefer, chocolate or turtle?"

"Turtle."

"I will check this spot near my house to see what time they close." Rico began performing an internet search for the office hours of the location. He noticed that the location closed at 7 p.m. so he wrote the address to program into his GPS later. "I'm going to have to enroll in some cooking classes. I can't have you cooking for me all the time; I'm a real man. All you need to do is come home and let me take care of you."

"Is that right?" Raegan had never heard such a thing. She was starting to think that he'd probably say just about anything to impress her. With wrinkled eyebrows, she said, "Sure, Rico…I believe you."

"I'm serious." He then began his campaign speech. "You will never have to cut your grass, pump your gas, wash the dishes, clean the carpet, change a tire; this list is pretty long, I just want you to know that I am a hard worker."

"Okay Rico. I have to go. Give me a call when you are on your way over. Okay?" Raegan pulled the phone away from her ear and shook her head.

"Will do."

After she replaced the receiver, she began to think how impossible he could be although sometimes cute. He could be flattering as well. She still wasn't quite sure what to make of him. Tonight would be another good opportunity for them to sit down to talk.

That evening Raegan began to prepare one of her favorite dishes, lemon peppered tilapia, rice pilaf and asparagus. It was a special recipe that she'd perfected about a year ago. She was craving the dish a few years back, after seeing a TV chef prepare it, so she decided to look up a recipe online. She had been preparing the dish for friends ever since then, and each of them liked it. Since it was such a hit with the rest of her friends, she decided to prepare it tonight. It was quite simple and she didn't have a lot of time to work in the kitchen that day, especially for someone she didn't know very well. However, she liked to entertain so she volunteered to have him over to give them time to get to know each other a little better. She was heading out of town to visit friends for a few days and then on to Florida for work, so this would give them time together before she left.

About one hour into her cooking, the doorbell rang.

Raegan made sure that everything was fine in the kitchen before she went to the door. "I see you found my place okay," she said with a bright, welcoming smile.

"Yeah, it's only about twenty minutes away from my place," Rico said as he entered her house. He leaned forward and kissed her cheek. "It smells really good in here. What are you cooking?" Rico asked as he took a moment to inhale the sweet aroma flowing from the kitchen.

"You will see and taste in just a moment," she said, playfully touching his nose.

As he walked into the tiled living room, he noticed the modern mismatched, yet coordinated furniture. He was surprised at her taste in furniture as it really didn't seem like her. The house looked pretty expensive, so that made him wonder how much money she earned working in HR. As he walked farther into the living room, he noticed the tray ceilings and arch doorways. The open floorplan also drew attention to the kitchen, which had beautiful stainless steel appliances with her sorority colors as the color scheme for kitchen accessories.

"This home is beautiful, just like the owner," Rico commented.

"Thanks. If you like, I can give you a quick tour," she asked after checking on the food once more.

"I'd love to see what you've done with the rest of the house," he said, taking her up on her offer.

Raegan led him down the hallway into the game room, where there were no games.

"I'd really like to get a pool table in here, but those things are so expensive," she said as she gave the tour.

"I know. It would be really nice in here though." Rico momentarily imagined himself in the game room, sitting in a leather chair, watching football on a fifty-inch flat screen.

"To the left is one guest bathroom; these two adjoining rooms are guest bedrooms. The master suite is on the other end of the hallway."

"This is really nice. How long have you been here?"

"For about ten months. God has certainly blessed me. Sometimes I still cannot believe I own a house," she said escorting him back to the kitchen.

"The food is just about ready. Please have a seat at the table and I will fix our plates shortly. Now, please be honest with me about the taste of the food. I like to cook, so I don't mind constructive criticism," she said as she removed plates from the cabinet.

"Of course," Rico said as he took his seat at the dining table. He was hungry so he was eager to taste the food regardless of how tasty or tasteless it was. His eyes and mouth began to water.

"Are you okay? Why are you teary-eyed?" Raegan asked with a confused look on her face.

"I'm tearing up because you are so wonderful. After all of my downfalls, God still saw enough in me to bless me with an angel like you, and that's simply amazing to me."

Raegan felt uncomfortable because she had a grown man tearing up in her kitchen and she hadn't done or said anything to cause it. "You better stop it right now," Raegan said in a playful voice to lighten the moment.

"I haven't shed a tear in so long that I think I have forgotten how. Anyway, let's eat because I'm starved."

Raegan was relieved when the awkward moment passed. She began to set the table so that they could eat. As they ate, they discussed their families, work and college careers. They had quite a few things in common, which made both of them even more interested in each other.

Raegan was becoming quite surprised at how her interest was growing in Rico. During dinner, Rico asked Raegan to date him exclusively so that they could *see where it goes* and she agreed. Rico convinced her that they would forever be getting to know each other and they could do that while they were in a relationship.

Moments after dinner, they bid their goodbyes and Raegan began to pack for her trips over the next week.

On the ride home, Rico thought about how well things were going with Raegan. He really enjoyed spending time with her and hoped that he could keep his past and present hidden while he continued getting to know her.

CHAPTER 9

∞

After dinner with Rico, Raegan left town on a red eye flight to participate in the homecoming festivities in Virginia with her sorority sisters. Jasmine, her favorite sorority sister, picked her up from the airport. Raegan immediately crashed on an air mattress when she arrived at Jasmine's apartment.

Jasmine's loud voice, coupled with the sun rays peeping through the faux wood blinds, woke her up later that morning. "Good morning!" Jasmine said. Her voice was naturally loud so Raegan couldn't snooze a few extra minutes if she wanted to.

"Hey, what's going on? What's for breakfast?" Raegan asked with a smile. She added, "Where is Kensi? I thought she came in last night?" Raegan continued stretching and yawning to shake off the fogginess of sleep.

"She did. She's in the shower getting ready, as you should be if we're going to make it to the game in enough time to tailgate."

"Great! I'll get ready after Kensi frees up the bathroom. Where is your laptop? I need to check my e-mail really quick to make sure nothing is needed from me at work."

"Child, aren't you off work? Clearly you don't know the meaning of a vacation. Vacation means e-mails and phones are off," Jasmine admonished her.

"I know, I know. I just like to check anyway to be sure there isn't a real emergency." Raegan wasn't actually concerned about work. She was secretly hoping that there would be an e-mail from Rico, as he seemed to e-mail her daily these days. She paused and smiled when she opened her inbox and saw that the last e-mail was from him:

Good morning,

I have been sitting here for hours just thinking about you. I must tell you again that you are absolutely amazing! I actually went to sleep thinking about you and woke up with you on my mind. I would say it's been a long time since I felt this way, but that would be a lie, I have never felt this way. I don't even have words to describe how I feel; you are so wonderful and so is this feeling. All I can do is thank GOD for meeting you, seriously. GOD I THANK YOU for seeing enough in me to send me one of your angels! I see so much when I look into your eyes, it's so comforting! WOMAN where have you been all my life, but then again I am glad you came at this time, a time when I have renewed myself as a man, and all the man I am, you now have. I have no reservations in giving myself to you, none whatsoever! In short I will say this, you are missed and thank you for giving my heart another function other than pumping blood. Can't wait until your return.

> *Rico*

Raegan was quickly interrupted by Jasmine's loud voice and a giggling Kensi. "Ma'am, why are you over there grinning? Surely there is nothing from work that will cause your face to light up like a Christmas tree and your teeth to show like you're getting ready for a cleaning!" Jasmine stood with one hand on her hip, sassily wagging the other hand.

"It's an e-mail from Rico. He is so sweet," Raegan said, blushing and sporting a school-girl grin. Raegan decided that since she had a couple of minutes, she would shoot him a quick e-mail before getting into the shower.

She knew things were moving quickly but that didn't stop her growing excitement. She felt like he could really be the one. Although she didn't know much about him and had only known him for a little while, she wanted to believe that he was sincere in his pursuit.

As Raegan sashayed away from the computer, heading toward the shower, Jasmine stopped her. "Now Rae, you know I want all of the deets now! That shower is going to have to wait! I want to know every single detail about how you met him and what has been going on. Don't leave anything out," Jasmine spoke excitedly, pulling Raegan by the hand back toward the caramel microfiber sofa.

"Now, you just finished trying to rush me into the shower and now that you want some juice, you've changed your mind, huh?" Raegan said teasing her.

"Yep! Now spill!" Jasmine said, sitting down beside her cuddling an olive green sofa pillow. Kensi slid her small frame onto the sofa as well to hear the story all over again. As Raegan recounted the details to Jasmine, Kensi occasionally stepped in to include details that Raegan left out.

"I haven't seen Raegan this excited before. We've got to meet this kid. What do you think Kensi?" Jasmine said as she moved away from the sofa to her vanity table to begin applying her make-up. Jasmine didn't necessarily have a good feeling about all of this, nor did she have a bad feeling. She couldn't quite put her finger on what was bothering her so she decided she would just let things play out as they should, since her girlfriend seemed so happy, but she would insist on meeting him soon.

CHAPTER 10

∞

Raegan enjoyed losing herself in the homecoming activities. She managed to enjoy the game and catch up with many classmates that she hadn't seen since graduation. There was one person that she didn't see, and that was Caleb. Although they hadn't spoken since their break-up back in college, a small part of her wanted to see him, to know how he was doing. She thought it was best that she didn't see him, though. She had so many mixed emotions after all of that time and wouldn't even know how to interact with him. Would she scream at him or squeeze him as if she didn't want to let go? She pushed her thoughts aside as she and her friends went out for dinner after their football team's huge win against the Gators.

Apparently her sisters couldn't wait to bring up the subject of Raegan and the guy she was currently dating, because as soon as they were seated at the dinner table, they began shooting questions at her. They attempted to do some questioning during the game but it was difficult with fans cheering and marching bands playing. One would swear they were a bunch of attorneys the way they grilled her.

"Well, I will just tell you guys what I think of him so far. Please keep in mind that we have only been dating for a short time." Almost as if a river burst through a dam, the words came spilling from her mouth in excitement. "He thinks I'm awesome; he constantly tells me about how awesome and amazing I am. He truly adores me and encourages me in everything. He has just been very positive and thinks that I am everything that he has prayed for in a wife. Every time I look up, he wants to spend time with me. I think that he can possibly be the one; however, there is a small voice telling me to slow down and pay attention to him because he is telling me everything that I want to hear. I keep telling myself that it's most likely fear and to let myself go."

Her sorority sisters smiled and nodded, encouraging Raegan to continue.

"I just think it's pretty amazing that he wants to spend the rest of his life with me. He seems pretty sure about it, so I asked him why he was so sure. He told me that the defining moment for him was when I got on my knees to pray at church. At that moment, he said that he knew I was the one."

"Well Raegan, if that's the case and you're happy, then I'm happy. However, not one time did you mention how *you* felt about this guy. How do you feel about him? Do you think as highly of him as he thinks of you? Do you think he may be the one? Do you think he's God sent? Do you think he's amazing and awesome?" Jasmine continued her questioning. "Does he have a good reputation? Who are his friends? Is a hard worker? Are you two equally yoked? Is he a strong Christian, without serious besetting sins? Does he do anything that will hinder your walk with God?" Jasmine spoke with concern and question in her eyes. She would be genuinely happy for her friend if she truly believed that this was what she wanted. She believed that Raegan was excited about the idea of a relationship with the guy and not necessarily excited about him. She liked the feeling that he gave her. Jasmine tried to hide her skepticism, but Raegan could feel it in her questioning.

"I wouldn't say that I think he's amazing, but the things he says are amazing. I think he's bold and confident, possibly bordering on the side of arrogance. I will have to get back to you on the other stuff but, overall, I think he's a good guy." Raegan hadn't quite taken the time to sit down to think about many of Jasmine's questions. She just knew how he made her smile, and that was important to her.

***

With homecoming over and a full week of training behind her, Raegan arrived at the airport, went through the usual check-in procedures, and located a coffee shop to

61

purchase her favorite cup of coffee. When she got to her terminal, she sat down to relax and drink her coffee. She thought about Rico and decided to send him an e-mail instead of calling since it was very early in the morning:

Hey,

As I sit here in the airport, listening to this new John Legend (which is totally awesome, I must add), I think about you. I just wanted to say "Good Morning" and wish you a great day!

As if you don't know already, you are such a great man...one of the many reasons I like you. I must admit that it is very difficult not to. (smiley face) It warms my heart to know that you see me in this "magic" light; it makes me want to be a better person.

Even though I've only known you for a short time, I have enjoyed getting to know you. If I've never told you, you are special.

Have a great day at work today! I look forward to seeing you soon.

Raegan

After sending the e-mail, she placed her headphones in her ear to listen to her iPod and relax a little until her plane arrived. The relaxing sounds of her favorites played softly in her ears as she sat watching passengers enter and exit the boarding gates throughout the busy airport.

When the airline representative announced that her plane had arrived, she began to gather her things in preparation for boarding when her section was called. She refreshed the page of her e-mail and noticed that Rico had already responded:

Hello,

I must admit that this was the perfect start to my day, I can't stop smiling. Seriously. If you only knew where I come from as far as relationships, you would understand why I am so honored to have you in my life.

There is not one moment in the day when I am not thinking about you and our future. I know the time has been short, but honestly this is what I have waited my entire life for and the time doesn't even matter to me. I know that you are for me, and I for you, and no amount of time, one day or one year is going to stop me from doing what I am supposed to do, and that is marry the woman of my dreams.

So again thank you for making my dream a reality.

As she read the e-mail a second time, she thought, *He sure knows how to lay it on thick.* It brought a smile to her face and left it there throughout the entire flight. She spent the flight daydreaming about him and what their relationship was going to be like. She spent time speaking silently to God wondering if He'd answered her prayer about sending "the one." Once again, the small voice warned her about continuing in a relationship with Rico. He was just so great that she was almost positive that it was fear speaking. She tossed the voices of fear out of the window and decided that she would take a chance on the relationship with him. After all, he was a nice Christian man.

As soon as she arrived at the airport and retrieved her luggage, Rico called. She knew it was him before she even looked at the caller ID. He didn't have a distinguished ringtone but she could just feel it. He'd been telling her that he missed her way before she even left the city.

"Hey darling!" she answered in a sing-song voice as she traveled across the parking garage to her car. It was windy outside and she was wearing a dress. So it was quite a task for her to drag her rolling suitcase, hold the phone and try to keep her dress from flying up in the wind.

"How are you sweetie?"

"Happy to be back on Texas soil," she said excitedly, echoing his words to her just a few days ago.

"That makes two of us. I'm glad you arrived safely. I thank God for another answered prayer."

"Yeah…" she responded with exhaustion. She was picking up her 40 pound suitcase and trying to place it in the trunk while trying to keep everything else in place.

"Are you okay over there? Why are you breathing like that?" he said with a light chuckle.

"I'm fine. I just put my bags in the car. I'm leaving the airport as we speak." Her coupe was small. She loved the style of her BMW, but sometimes she became annoyed with the fact that she only had two doors. If she had four doors, she could have just tossed her luggage into the backseat.

"Oh okay. I just finished telling my best friend about you. Everyone is so in love with you! I e-mailed my other friend a picture of you today and he thinks you're gorgeous!" Rico said with excitement and contentment now that Raegan received his friends' approval, not that he needed it considering he was the only person who could really decide what was right for him.

"Well that is nice of them. Tell them I said thank you." Raegan was used to receiving compliments on her dark, shiny, curly locks that flowed to the middle of her back. Raegan smiled as she buckled her seatbelt. "All right Rico, I will see you later on tonight when you leave work."

"I can't wait!" he said as they ended the call.

CHAPTER 11

∞

Rico loved his job but he didn't feel like he was being paid what he was worth, especially with the additional duties that he'd been performing as of late. As someone new to car sales, he had high hopes for himself and his career. His friends were all married with lucrative careers, earning six-figure salaries. Coming close to what his friends earned and having the type of lifestyle that each of them had was his dream. Somehow, he felt like this would validate his manhood and fill the emptiness that he felt inside. Raegan earned a higher salary than he did, especially in a month when he didn't sell any cars at all, so getting a promotion and salary increase was now more important than ever. He needed to continue spending time with and doing nice things for Raegan in addition to other long-term commitments; the only way he believed he could support his lifestyle was to earn more money.

Thankful that his workday was over and Raegan had returned to town, Rico planned a special evening with her, knowing that he would be able to spend more time with her than just the usual couple of hours.

Raegan was suffering from minor jetlag and didn't want to go out, so Rico brought over dinner from Boston Market. As they sat in her kitchen eating, he began to express his feelings to her.

"I have something to say to you and I hope it doesn't scare you." He was hoping that his confession would bring them closer together, keep her from becoming suspicious and even weaken her resolve not to engage in pre-marital sex.

With a chuckle, she tossed her glossy curls away from her face and spoke. "You're actually making me nervous by saying that." She always felt that way whenever people attempted to prep her before speaking. She would much rather the person just say what was on their mind instead of using phrases like, "Can I tell you something?" or "If I tell you this will you be upset?" or "I have something to tell you." Those phrases made her skin crawl. "Go on. Just say it." She gave him her full attention, placing her fork on her plate and looking him in the eyes.

"Raegan, I really like you, more than I should I think. I don't want to force anything on you or put you in an uncomfortable position, but I see everything I want in you and will do all in my power to build us a solid foundation and build a house of marriage." As much as he really wanted to do this, he knew that he couldn't give that kind of life to Raegan right now. That didn't stop how he felt though. But maybe just saying it would be enough to keep her interested.

"You've told me that before, so that isn't anything new." It didn't make her nervous but it did scare her just an *insy winsy* bit. She wasn't sure if he should be feeling like that, but some say that "when you know, you just know."

"I know but I just wanted to tell you again," he said as he brushed a stray curl away from her face.

She was halfway excited and halfway worried about his declaration. He seemed sincere but something just didn't feel right—although the feeling wasn't uncomfortable enough to make her stop seeing him. She ignored it and chose to live in the moment.

After dinner, Rico and Raegan sat on her sofa, talking and laughing and playing card games. The later it became, the more Rico became more *touchy*. He rubbed Raegan's feet while listening to her talk about her family and her childhood dreams. He even shared some personal stories of his own. Slowly, the mood shifted. He traded foot rubs for kisses, melting away Raegan's resolve. Raegan eventually succumbed to his subtle advances and before she knew it, she had broken her vow.

Raegan sent Rico home and the realization of what she allowed to happen set in. What had she done? She had done the very thing that she promised God, herself and her accountability partner that she wouldn't do. For two years, she had been able to show restraint and focus on her relationship with her Heavenly Father; and in a matter of moments, she let it go.

Sulking over her transgression, she curled up on the couch and cried, repeatedly saying *Lord, please forgive me.* She experienced a myriad of emotions. She felt dirty and used. Confusion and heartache also filled her heart. She got caught up in the moment, believing Rico's promise to someday marry her. She rationalized that because he would soon be her husband, it was all right. *This can't happen again,* she thought. *I need to get myself together.*

CHAPTER 12

∞

Ding dong, ding dong, ding dong. *Only Tammy would play with the doorbell like that*, Raegan thought as she headed to answer the door. As Raegan walked across the cold tile floors to the door, she was reminded that she needed to turn on the heat. The temperature was dropping, as evidenced by her cold toes.

"Party time!" Tammy screamed as she stepped through the door. "Am I the first to arrive?" she asked, holding up a bottle of Chavignon Blanc.

"Yes, you are, and I'm surprised considering you're usually late. You must have been out of the house running errands or something?" Raegan asked, raising an eyebrow as she embraced her friend.

"Actually, I just left the hair salon. My bags were already packed so I decided to come on over after stopping to pick up a nice bottle of bubbly to help with our 'moment of truth' discussion," she said, winking at Raegan.

Just as they walked into the kitchen to chill the bottle of wine, Michelle rang the doorbell. "Don't worry Rae," Tammy said. "I'll get it. It's probably Shelly." Shelly was Tammy's nickname for Michelle.

"Only you would wear shades in November! You just have to be fly at all times, don't you?" Tammy asked giving Michelle a hug. "I think the last time I saw you, you were still with Jason." Michelle rolled her eyes while playfully pushing Tammy's shoulder.

"You're ready to start something, aren't you? Rae, did you give Tammy any wine? You know she doesn't need any truth serum," Michelle tossed the words over her shoulder, leaving Tammy at the door.

"She just walked in the door about five minutes before you showed up. She hasn't had anything yet," Raegan said, pointing to the unopened bottle of wine.

Sauntering into the kitchen in her purple chiffon blouse and black pencil skirt, Michelle looked as though she had just left a photo shoot for *Vogue* magazine's successful, sexy and professional issue. "Rae it smells good in here! What are we having tonight?" Michelle asked while lifting the top off the crock pot. She switched on the oven light and tried to take a peek at what was cooking.

Tammy and Michelle both slid out of their shoes and sat around the large kitchen island talking with Raegan as she finished dinner.

"So what's going on?" Michelle and Tammy asked in unison, both eager to catch up.

"No deal," Raegan said as she waved her wooden spoon at them. "Now you all know that we can't start this until—" *ding dong*. The doorbell interrupted her before she could finish her sentence. "I'll be right back."

Raegan returned singing, "Guess who's here!" as she ushered Kensi into the kitchen.

"Ahhhh! Hey girl! Rae, you didn't tell us that Kensi would be in town! This is definitely going to be a fun night," said Michelle excitedly. Kensi would be coming on assignment for work next week, so she decided to come early to spend the weekend with her girls. Kensi went to college with Raegan. Michelle and Tammy, she met through Raegan.

The four friends gathered around the island to discuss men, money, work, dreams and the like. Each one of them had many stories to tell and a plethora of advice to give and receive. They were likely to not get any sleep that night.

Raegan's friends were eager to hear about the juicy details of Raegan and Rico's whirlwind romance. Raegan placed the plates in front of them, prayed over the food, slid onto a bar stool and began discussing her relationship with Rico. Likes, dislikes and worries.

"You all already know the basics. How and where we met and the sweet letters that he sends just about every day," she said gesturing with her hands as if to say "blah, blah, blah." Rico was quite the gentleman, opening doors, pulling out her chair, standing when she needed to be excused from the dinner table, giving her his coat when she was cold, holding her hand to assist her up and down stairs and all nice things like that. However, Raegan still had some serious concerns and was hoping that her friends could help her sort it all out.

Raegan did not want to go into the issue of having broken her celibacy with Rico because her friends would definitely not allow the conversation to continue for questions as to why, when and where. Their statements and questions would remind her of how she messed up and she didn't want to deal with it. So she decided she would keep that tidbit of information to herself although she knew she needed to confess it because it was weighing on her chest like heartburn.

"So here is the biggest issue," Raegan said dramatically. "He does a lot of talking about us getting married in the near future, but there is a money issue. At least for me. This dude sends his mom $1,500 per month, which is a pretty hefty chunk of money, no matter how much he earns. He has never really addressed why; the only thing he has said about it is that she has taken care of him all of her life and that he wants to do the same for her." As if on cue, her friends all shouted things like "No way!" "You're lying!"

"Now, I know that's his momma but I am definitely not comfortable with that. Based off conversations that we've had, I get the impression that he feels obligated to do this for her and he seems to be bothered by it. He complains about helping her out but then says she doesn't really need his help. To add to that, she is supposed to be a pastor. I always thought that churches make sure their pastors are taken care of, especially when it comes to living expenses. It just sounds fishy to me." Raegan took a bite of food to let her words sink in.

"Right," Michelle slowly chimed in. "You know my father is a pastor and the church gives him a salary and a housing allowance, so he could be misleading you in some way. I know that all churches do not have the ability to support their pastor so it just depends on the size and financial obligations of the church. I'm still a little skeptical though. Something about their situation doesn't sound right."

"Exactly!" Raegan said putting emphasis on the *ex*. "I mean, really. Who does that? There is no issue with sending a relative money because they need it, but there is an issue with sending anyone $1,500 per month regularly and you're acting as if you're hardly making ends meet yourself. So that concerns me a lot and I'm planning to have a conversation with him about it. Do you all think it's too soon to talk with him about things like that?"

Tammy couldn't wait to chime in. "No way. Do it as soon as possible. If he is serious about wanting to marry you, then there shouldn't be an issue with him being open and honest with you about his finances. In fact, you both need to pull your credit reports and review them together. The last thing you want to do is get into a marriage with someone and later get hit with a boomerang of financial issues because you didn't do your due diligence." Tammy's advice came from the standpoint of someone with an estranged husband. Her failed marriage often weighed heavily on her, and if she could help her friends not make the same mistake, she was all for it.

"You're certainly right about that Tam. I'm definitely going to bring it up," Raegan said, letting out a sigh of relief that at least her friends understood her issues; she just hoped that Rico would understand her feelings as well.

"I know you're about ready to move on to your next point but seriously, who does that?" Kensi asked with a confused look on her face. She had been sitting there listening intently and watching Raegan's body language. She could tell that this issue was really bothering Raegan. "I'm sitting here trying to sort through this while you're speaking and it just doesn't make sense. It sounds as if he is making an excuse for his poor financial situation. Maybe he's made some bad choices and potentially trying to clear them up? Or maybe he's still making bad financial choices."

"Gambling? Drugs? Another woman?" Kensi continued as she thought about the possibilities. She and Raegan shared similar thoughts on most issues, so she was only asking the questions that Raegan dared not ask herself. She secretly hoped that it was none of those issues because he seemed like such a great guy. She thought he could be *the one*.

"Thanks ladies for helping me think through this and giving me other things to think about," she said as she raised her eyebrows at Kensi. "We've been dating a couple of months now and things are moving pretty quickly. Now again, he is talking a lot about marriage, and I'm concerned that he has never invited me over to his apartment. Besides, he has been to my place on numerous occasions," Raegan explained, *and has even stayed overnight,* she added to herself.

"Really? We're all thirty-somethings and have been in quite a few relationships. There is obviously something wrong with this picture!" Kensi said emphatically. "Rae, how can you even consider marrying this dude and you've never been to his place? Does he even have a place? For all you know, he may be living with another woman."

Raegan's body stiffened at the thought of Rico betraying her in such a way, especially after everything she'd shared with him – her time *and* her body.

"Maybe he is trying to move into this nice big place you have," Michelle said giggling, as she raised her hand in a gesture to show off Raegan's lovely home.

"Yeah…that's what bothers me. It just all seems so weird. I'm almost in one of those *he's too good to be true* situations," Raegan said as she mindlessly tapped the table. "I suppose I'm still dating his representative. He is doing a very good job at portraying who he would like me to think he is. I guess I really need to think more critically about him and get the hearts out of my eyes, huh?" she said darting her eyes at Kensi who she knew would have something to add.

"What?" Kensi asked while taking a sip of her glass of wine. "I didn't say a word. Rae, you're smart and you already know what you need to do. You don't need any of us to tell you that," Kensi said, waving her hand around to each friend. "I will say this though. Be smart about it. Don't get so caught up with all of the sweet things he's whispering into your ear. See the relationship for what it is because right now, all he's giving you is lip service. He is telling you he wants to marry you but he hasn't actually done anything to show you that. I know you're all in love with him right now and you're probably not even hearing anything I'm saying to you, but stay on your toes," Kensi said and sipped her wine again.

"Well," Tammy said. "Kensi just about summed it up for you. If you're having doubts about him, don't be so quick to accept everything he is saying to you. I know you started off being tough with him, but you started to ease up when you thought he was the man that God sent to you. Even if that is true, he still has to work for you. He still needs to prove himself. You need to take the time to get to know buddy, because something in the water isn't clean and it's bound to reveal itself soon. I just hope your eyes are open sweetie," Tammy said as she walked around the large granite island to give Raegan a hug.

"If this is the real deal, we are all very happy for you; just don't ignore the red flags. Trust your intuition," Michelle said. She could attest to relationships going wrong fast with three failed engagements under her belt.

CHAPTER 13

∞

As the ladies placed their plates in the dishwasher and refilled their wine glasses, Michelle shared her failed engagement with her friends to air out her feelings.

"Jason and I are now finished. Raegan and I work together so she already knows the story, but I will share my problems anyway," Michelle said as they all left the kitchen and gathered into the living room to recline on Raegan's sage green sofas and La-Z-Boy chairs.

"Against my better judgment, we moved in together. Things were going great in the beginning, of course, but one day he came back to the apartment after work with such a nasty attitude. It was the first time I'd ever seen him like that," Michelle said, flailing her hands in the air. "I swear it seemed like he had lost his mind," she continued. "Every little thing was setting him off. For example, while I was cooking, I burned the dinner rolls.

They were still edible but he fussed about that. I asked him to help me out by washing the dishes after dinner. He fussed about that. He was bringing my mood down so much that particular night that I decided to go to bed early. That was just the beginning of everything turning sour. During one of our pre-marital counseling sessions, he admitted that part of his issue is that we stopped having sex. That really pisses me off because we mutually agreed to stop having sex shortly after we became engaged," she paused to take a sip of wine. "I thought we were both on the same page with trying to live better lives before God but obviously not! Ugh!" Michelle said, exasperated.

"Hold on, wait!" Tammy interrupted. "Now you know that you can't give dude the cookie before you get engaged and then just decide to take it away," Tammy said giggling. "I mean, seriously. You can't blame him too much for getting upset about that. Here you were, having sex with him, get engaged to marry, then you snatch the cookie away as if you were using it as bait. Guys love sex, honey, and they generally feel like they're moving backwards if you're taking it away, even if you're about to get married." Tammy snapped her fingers to solidify her point.

Raegan's stomach twisted into knots at Tammy's reasoning because of how she'd let herself go with Rico. She was already feeling guilty enough about what happened between the two of them and now her friend was sitting here saying there was no going back. *But Tammy wasn't Rico*, she thought.

Echoing Raegan's thoughts, Michelle sat up straight on the couch and interjected, "Well hold on for a second now. So you're saying that if a woman slips up and says yes once, twice or lots of times, then she can't ever say no? What if she decides that it's wrong and she wants to do the right thing by waiting until marriage? Then what?"

"A woman is certainly allowed to say *no* whenever she wants but you should understand that a guy may feel like he's moving backwards and that usually doesn't end well unless he agrees that the sex should wait until marriage," Tammy said to clarify her point.

"Can it really be serious enough to throw our relationship away?" Michelle asked as her eyes began to water, becoming frustrated again.

"I'm sorry honey, but I don't make the rules. If you want to wait until you get married, you can't give it up at all," Tammy said as she moved over to sit next to Michelle. She could see that her words were really getting to her. Tammy rubbed Michelle's back as the tears fell. Tammy continued, "Guys are like this. They simply want the cookies. If we give them up, they are going to expect to keep getting them. To them, they are receiving mixed signals if we give it up and then take it away. I know it's hard to wait, but you have to make a choice. We've all had this conversation before. We want God's blessings on our marriage whenever we get married, so we are trying to hold on to the cookies until then. Establish the boundaries up front and stick to them like our girl Rae over here," she said as she winked at Rae.

Rae avoided making eye contact with any of them at that moment because she wasn't sticking to her guns these days. Instead, she repositioned herself in the chair to help alleviate the awkwardness she felt in that moment.

"I understand all of that, but I felt like we had a connection. Another reason why I wanted to stop having sex is because I didn't want to pretend like I was already his wife. He was receiving too many marital benefits without us yet having tied the knot. I was cooking for him, laundering his clothes and rolling around in the bed with him at night. I was just beginning to feel like we were doing too much. The pastor confirmed my feelings during our pre-marital counseling session when he stated that we were putting marital pressures on our relationship by living together and acting like we were married," Michelle explained.

"Wow. I like the way he expressed that. That's good info right there," Kensi chimed in. It made her think of some of her own failed relationships. Although she had never lived with anyone, she had played the role of a wife.

"Yeah, so marriage counseling helped bring out a lot of sore spots in our relationship. We broke up after that particular session. We just felt like we didn't have what it took to make a marriage work. We weren't apart for long. Two days after breaking up, Jason called me at work, apologizing and wanting to work through our issues. I love him so I decided to take him back without question," Michelle said, as her friends stared intently at her, coaxing her with their eyes to continue.

"We went to the park to talk things through but that didn't end well at all. Our conversation quickly turned into an argument as I asked him to set a wedding date. He just could not commit to a date and I was getting so frustrated with him. His indecisiveness was driving me insane. The more we talked, the more the conversation began to get heated as he expressed how he only agreed to stop having sex just to please me but he couldn't deal with it. It was something about the way that he said it that gave me pause. The next thing I knew, the palm of my hand met his right cheek! I knew right then that he'd cheated!!"

Michelle's admission was quickly met with questions from her friends as to how she knew Jason was cheating and if she ever confirmed that it was true.

"Yes! I was so pissed. So Tammy, I guess your theory is right. He had to have it; his shameful tail just couldn't keep his stick in his pants. It was officially over then. I threw his ring at his head and it landed somewhere along the bike trail. Who knows and who cares? But as quickly as they go, they come."

"What do you mean?" Raegan asked mid sip.

"You know exactly what I mean. I'm over it. I'm glad I didn't marry his cheating behind. I'm taking a time-out on relationships to focus on what Michelle wants."

"Just slow down the next time you get into a relationship, OK?" Raegan said. "You just ended your third engagement. What are you doing to these guys to get them to propose anyway?"

"Rae, you know the answer to that question," Kensi said chuckling. "She is giving up the cookie. I guess you can't be an Indian giver with the cookie. It's not working for Michelle." The room erupted with laughter and it was just what everyone needed to lighten the mood.

"Ah, hush girl," Michelle said to Kensi while playfully tagging her with a sofa pillow. "So who are you not giving the cookie to these days?"

"First of all, can we stop saying *cookie*? Secondly, I'm not really involved with anyone. My efforts these days are focused on becoming editor-in-chief!" The job would go to either her or her colleague, Michael. Kensi felt as if she had to work twice as hard being a woman, so she did just that. She covered the best stories and stayed on top of any training that she could get.

"Y'all know I spend most of my time traveling for work. I don't have much time for anything else these days and that is all right with me," Kensi said pointing to herself. Kensi had been fully focused on her career since her relationship failed with Zach. Zach was Kensi's first love.

The only reason they broke up is that they accepted jobs in different parts of the country and didn't work hard enough to make their long distance relationship work.

She had dated a few guys since then, as her way of acting out her frustration with Zach, but nothing serious. When she saw that none of those relationships were going anywhere, and her life was spiraling out of control, she decided to make a change for the better; that is when she and Raegan made their celibacy pact.

CHAPTER 14

∞

Tammy was once married for one year to her college sweetheart, Joshua. They married during their senior year in college, while on Christmas break. Both were young and hopeful that their relationship would last forever, but without marital counseling or more mature married couples to mentor them, their relationship did not make it through the fire. Unlike some couples who were still experiencing the honeymoon phase during the first year of marriage, it was a time of turmoil and heartbreak for Tammy and Joshua.

Joshua was their university's basketball team's MVP. Most sports analysts predicted that he was a sure pick for the NBA draft. After marrying during the Christmas holiday, his final collegiate basketball career was in full swing and he vowed not to allow anything or anyone get in the way of him achieving his dream of making it to the NBA. He was sure that Tammy was on board with him achieving his dream.

Just as everyone predicted, Joshua went on to the NBA, but he lost Tammy in the process. In Tammy's eyes, his lack of attention to her needs, constant traveling and total disregard for her own dreams almost immediately tore their relationship apart when his NBA career began. Tammy decided early on that their marriage would always be about him and what he wanted and that they should end it before things got ugly.

From Joshua's perspective, separation was not the answer. He loved Tammy and thought they were planning to build a life together. He thought she would be able to handle his career and what it would require of him, especially as a rookie, but she remained selfish and wanted more time with him as newlyweds. He didn't think the NBA was that much of a change from the amount of time required from him in school, except that once he received the contract, more traveling would be involved than before. He had even gone through the process of purchasing a house so that they could begin building their life together. Instead, she chose to move to Texas while he went on to pursue his career in Boston.

Some days, she regretted being immature and bailing on her marriage. She hadn't thought that being the wife of a pro basketball player would be so difficult. She always thought that when they were married, he would spend his time doting on her. Part of her understood that his career would be demanding, but a greater part of her wanted to be more important to him.

"I don't have nearly as much going on in my life as the three of you. I talk with Josh from time to time and that's about it. I still love him but I don't want to fight for his attention," she said, moving down to the floor in front of the fireplace with the rest of her girls. "I've known him half of my life already. We dated through high school and college, and he is really the only guy that I have ever wanted to be married to." *But at what expense? Why do I have to be the one to give up everything while he gets to live his dreams?* she thought.

"On a much more serious note, I'd like you all to please be in prayer for my granny. She has been diagnosed with lung cancer." Knowing the possible outcome, Tammy became saddened. She pulled her knees to her chest and rested her chin. Her friends sat in silence as she made her request.

She reflected on the conversation she had while visiting with her grandmother earlier that week and that gave her a smile.

Tammy's grandmother said, "Just know that Granny has always loved you and I am so proud of the woman that you have become. Too bad that handsome lil' boy didn't stick around. He is still my grandbaby, even if things didn't work out between you two."

Her grandma was always bringing up Joshua, but she pretended as if she didn't know who Granny was referring to. "Who are you talking about, Granny?"

"You know exactly who I'm talking about. Josh. When is the last time you talked to him?"

"It's been a while. But let's not talk about him; I want to make sure you're okay," Tammy remembered saying.

"Oh, don't worry about me honey. Granny has lived and loved and you need to do the same. Promise Granny that you will call my grandson."

"Okay, I will," Tammy promised, not knowing when she would call.

"No, call him right now. I want to talk to him," her grandmother said as a way to make sure that Tammy would keep her promise. She knew that Tammy was stubborn and would probably never reach out to him although he made contact with her from time to time.

"Really, Granny? This is what you're worried about?" *Shouldn't you be more concerned about your health?* she thought.

"Get him on the phone, her grandmother said sternly."

Obeying her grandmother, she called Joshua. As soon as he picked up and they exchanged hellos, her grandma motioned for her to pass the phone.

"Hey baby."

"Hey Granny Rose. You don't sound very well. Are you okay?" Joshua was concerned.

Ignoring his question, she jumped right into the reason she wanted to talk to him.

"Honey, take it from me. You don't want to waste time being angry and upset and waging war about who is more important. It is time out for all of that. You two need to come to your senses and start working this out. She still loves you." Her grandmother had held her peace the entire time. Since she was now coming to terms with her mortality, she couldn't hold her tongue anymore. Someone needed to tell them to get their acts together, and she was just the right person for the job.

"Granny, we—" Tammy said, starting to interrupt her grandma, but she thought better of it when Granny gave her a sideways glance. She knew not to interrupt her grandmother when she was talking. She only wanted to say that they hadn't made any sort of plans to work anything out and she didn't know if they ever would.

Granny's words boosted Joshua's confidence. He wanted to work things out with her and see if they could ever get back to the point of being husband and wife again. He was glad that Granny Rose shared his thoughts.

"Tammy was the best thing that ever happened to me. The time apart has been rough on me, you know. Although I was able to build my basketball career, it was tough not having her by my side. But I promise I am going to do all that I can to make things work soon enough."

Granny smiled and said, "Thank you dear; that is all that I ask." Tammy couldn't hear what Joshua said to her Granny, but it must have been satisfactory because she was smiling. Her grandmother handed the phone back to her and she ended the call.

Tammy's thoughts were interrupted by the comfort of her friends. "We're so sorry Tammy," her friends all echoed.

"If there is anything that you need us to do, just say the word," Raegan said, having lost one of her grandmothers to lung cancer as well. "How is she doing?"

"She's still herself. She is eighty-two years old and set in her ways. She feels like she's lived the best years of her life and refuses to undergo chemotherapy," Tammy said as she thought about how the entire family disapproved of her grandmother's choice. Tammy's grandmother has been a smoker for as long as she knew and still had no plans to stop, even though she had been diagnosed with the disease.

"Be sure to love on her while she's still here. Try not to focus on this being the end and enjoy the time you guys have left," Raegan said as they all stood to cover Tammy and her family in prayer.

CHAPTER 15

∞

After breakfast, more sisterly discussion and prayer, they all said their good-byes and went their separate ways. Raegan decided to run errands. Before leaving, she received a call from Rico.

"Hello pretty lady," Rico's smooth voice echoed on the other end of the phone.

"Hey, how are you?" Raegan asked with a smile on her face.

"I'm great. Guess who's in town?"

"Your mother?" she asked. Rico never mentioned introducing her to his mother even though he seemed convinced he wanted to marry her. She asked once but he came up with an excuse as to why it would have to wait.

"No ma'am. She is not coming out here. She is scared to drive on the freeway." That was another one of

Rico's excuses to present a barrier as to why Raegan would not meet his mother.

"Well, tell me then."

"My best friend, Michael. He wants to meet you. I've told him all about you and he wants to see this beauty for himself."

"Way to rub on the butter. I may be able to meet you all somewhere. What do you have planned today?"

"We're headed to Buffalo Wild Wings to grab a quick bite to eat. I know its short notice, but can you swing by? We'll actually be at the location near your house," Rico went on, hoping that since they would be in her area, she would choose to attend.

"Well," she said dragging out the word. "Since you're going to be so close, I will stop by in between my errands. I can't stay to eat with you guys, I'm only coming in for a quick minute to say hello to your friend."

Raegan went to the dry cleaners and stopped by the grocery store to pick up a few items. She figured that by the time she finished those two things, they would have arrived and ordered their food. After returning the items to her house, she stopped by the restaurant.

As soon as Raegan entered the restaurant, she spotted the guys and her heart immediately fell to the floor. *Oh my world, what on earth is Caleb doing here?* she thought. Her stomach tightened, her throat became dry and she suddenly felt the need to use the restroom. How would she be able to go over to that table with Caleb sitting there? *What is he doing here? And with my boyfriend? This cannot be happening. This has to be some kind of joke.* She tried to think of any excuse not to walk over there, but before she could come up with anything, Rico spotted her. "Help me Lord," she prayed silently. It was a good thing she looked great while running her errands today. The weather was very nice for November so she was dressed in a beautiful royal purple cashmere sweater, form-fitting blue jeans and sassy peep-toe heels, with just enough opening to show off her freshly pedicured toes.

"Hey sweetie," Rico said as he gave her a hug and brushed a kiss on her cheek. Rico introduced her to his fraternity brothers –Michael and Caleb. They were in town for a fraternity convention.

Her body stiffened as she stood there in shock. She felt as if she was in a warp zone. *This cannot be happening. What are the odds?* She thought. She knew about the convention but had never expected to see Caleb.

Before Rico could finish the introductions, Caleb stood up and cut him off. "Raegan Camille Sanders!" he said with surprise and pleasure, never once taking his eyes off her, oblivious to both Michael and Rico.

"Caleb, how are you?" she asked as politely as she could. Her eyes flashed with a myriad of emotions. Caleb and Raegan's history dated back to college. She loved him so much and he cheated on her with one of her sorority sisters. Although she wasn't very close to the sister, the pain didn't sting any less. After his profession of love, he demonstrated it by pulling his pants down with anyone who would open her legs to him. The feelings of disgust and anger were beginning to return, but she decided she would not give him the satisfaction.

"Michael, it is great to meet you. How are you?" she asked with a brighter, more sincere smile, extending her hand to him. "I've heard so much about you. It's nice to meet you. How is your wife?" Raegan turned to Michael in an attempt to civilly dismiss Caleb.

"She's doing great. I will tell her that I met you while I was here. She wanted to come down and shop while I attended the convention activities, but she had plenty of work to catch up on."

"I can understand that. How long are you here? I may be able to catch up with you guys some time later, but I really have a ton of things that I need to finish before today is over," she said, trying to forget that Caleb was even present. But she could feel his eyes burning a hole through her skull. He remained standing, relishing in the moment although he sensed she was still harboring a grudge against him.

"I won't have much time after today. I'm actually planning on traveling back home early to be with my lovely wife."

"How sweet is that?!" she said, winking at Rico. "Please take notes from Michael over here. He seems to have the right idea. He could be a good influence on you in the future," Raegan playfully tagged his chest.

"Taking notes ma'am," Rico said as he took air notes in his hand. Pulling her closer to him, he asked, "So how do you know Caleb? I just met him today." Rico had noticed the look in Caleb's eyes when looking at Raegan. He could tell that Caleb had feelings for her and that didn't sit well with him. He knew that wasn't just some regular *hello* but there was definitely meaning behind it.

"We went to undergrad together." She was trying to dismiss the conversation, but Rico wasn't quite letting it go. "Bye Michael, I will see you again soon," she said and just waved good-bye to Caleb as she began walking away.

"It doesn't sound like you two just went to college together. He knows your full name. I don't think I even knew your middle name," Rico continued to press the issue as he walked her back to her car.

"We used to date," she said without any further explanation. "Can we not talk about this right now?" she asked. She needed time to gather her thoughts.

"All right now, I don't want any mess out of you young lady," he said smiling. "I'm going to head back inside. Please be safe. I will call you later," Rico said as he closed her car door. Rico somehow had the feeling that he was no longer the only one with secrets. The way Raegan and Caleb looked at each other caused a knot to develop in his stomach. He knew there was something going on and he planned to find out later.

"Will do," she mouthed to him as he walked away. She slid back into her coupe and proceeded to call Kensi. This was one call that just couldn't wait. She was trembling as she dialed the numbers. *Please pick up. Please pick up.* Unbeknownst to her, Caleb was walking outside looking for her, just as Rico went back inside. Caleb excused himself from the table to go to the restroom. Luckily for him, the restroom was close enough to the door, allowing him to exit without Michael and Rico noticing. He spotted her sitting in her coupe on the phone.

"Hello! What's going on? I thought you were out running errands?" Kensi said as she answered the phone.

"I was until I stopped to meet Rico and his friend at Buffalo Wild Wings. I'm about to have some sort of attack out here. You will never ever believe who was inside *and* sitting at the table with Rico!"

"One of your ex-beaus!" Kensi said jokingly.

"Yes!" Raegan shouted through the phone.

"I was only kidding. Who could it have been? You have so many."

"This is no time to be joking, Kensi. Caleb is here!!" After Raegan said his name, there was complete silence. Kensi was hardly ever at a loss for words but she didn't know what to say. She knew all about Raegan and Caleb's history. Raegan loved the guy and although she never said anything, Kensi was pretty convinced that he was part of the reason she left Damian at the altar a couple of years ago.

"So you aren't going to say anything?" Raegan asked, needing her friend to say something to help calm her down.

"What do you want me to say? I'm just as stunned as you are. What is he doing—? Oh wait, his fraternity convention is this weekend. What a small world! I didn't even think of that, let alone think that you would actually see him. Why was he with Rico?"

"Rico's best friend is a member of their fraternity as well. Apparently the best friend and Caleb met during the convention and he invited Caleb to come along for lunch…Why me?" Raegan whined. Glancing up, she saw Caleb. "Oh, no! Kens, this dude is standing in front of my car, motioning for me to get out and talk to him. What should I do?" Raegan asked, her voice almost a whisper. She spoke as if Caleb could hear her every word. That was an awkward question coming from Raegan, who was always so confident. She fumbled with the phone and dropped it on the floor.

"Well, you know I'm going to say go talk to him, and not because I think you really need to talk to him but because I want to know what he has to say. Just do it and call me back later. Love you," Kensi said and immediately hung up the phone to avoid protest or debate from Raegan.

Back inside the restaurant Michael questioned Rico's sanity. "What do you think you're doing man? Why are you leading Raegan on? She seems like such a beautiful woman."

"Dude, what are you talking about? I love Raegan."

"While that may be true in some odd way, you shouldn't be treating Chloe like this. She doesn't deserve it and neither does Raegan. And you have this woman believing that you are actually going to marry her. Do you not see how wrong that is?" Michael chastised him.

Rico assured Michael that everything would be fine and that Chloe would never find out. However, Michael warned him, "Man, you know you reap what you sow. And the next time, leave me out of it!" He didn't want any part of Rico's mischiefs. Michael loved his wife and didn't want her to have any doubt about his commitment to her because of Rico's issues.

"What about your vows? How do you plan to keep this secret from Raegan? As a matter of fact, why are you parading her around? Do you *want* to get caught?" Michael pressed him. He didn't agree with Rico's actions but he also thought that Rico wasn't even acting wisely while doing his dirt.

"Man, chill out! Chloe's nose is so far up in that hospital that she would never find out." Rico was confident that his transgressions would go undetected by Chloe because she worked long hours at the hospital.

"I'm just telling you that you're wrong." Michael shook his head. He didn't want to be involved in Rico's lies and warned him again to keep him out of it.

CHAPTER 16

∞

Caleb continued to beckon Raegan out of the car. There was no way he was going to miss an opportunity to talk with her now that he had laid eyes on her again. With sweaty and shaky palms, Raegan opened her car door and stood just inside the door without moving away from the car.

"So, what do you want?" she asked Caleb. She was so nervous that she swore she could hear the sound of her heart beating in her ears. It had been such a long time since she last saw him and she had such mixed emotions seeing him now. A part of her wanted to give him the biggest hug she could muster while the other part of her wanted to scream at him, releasing the frustration that she never released years ago when she broke up with him.

"You," he stated quite plainly and without any sign of a smile. He stood there staring into her eyes so intensely that Raegan could feel a stirring in the pit of her stomach.

"Caleb, please don't do this. What do you want? I don't have time for this," she said, becoming outwardly agitated but inwardly excited. She was stunned by his response. She was definitely not expecting to hear him say that, although a part of her welcomed the admission. There may have been some feelings lingering around for him. She did love him very much at one point, but that was until he hurt her. Deeply. She had to admit that a small part of her still wanted him, *always had*. Maybe it was to hurt him like he hurt her, or it could have very well been that she believed they were meant to be together.

"I know you believe what you thought you saw or heard that night but I wasn't even—"

"None of that matters anymore, Caleb!" she said, cutting him off, her voice slightly elevated. "What were you thinking? Wait, please don't answer that because I don't want to know. I don't want to hear any excuses. That was such a long time ago and we should both let it go, okay?" She didn't believe the words as she spoke them. The more he stood there in front of her, the more she wanted an explanation of what happened, hoping that it could somehow change things between them.

"Well, let's be fair Cami." He was the only one who ever called her by her middle name, and a shortened version of it at that. "You never really gave me a chance to explain. You slapped me and stormed off. You wouldn't accept my calls, any of my messages through your friends, and you wouldn't respond to my letters, e-mails or voicemails. You wouldn't even answer the door for me when I showed up to your place. What was I supposed to do? You walked out on me and didn't even think twice about giving us a chance. I really thought we had something," he paused for a moment, his eyes locked on hers. "If what we had was real, how could you be so quick to give up on us?" That was the question he pondered for years. How could she just walk out on their relationship like that?

"You're standing in front of me begging for me to slap you again! How can you say something like that? You were the one who gave up on us when you cheated! How could you be so cold to me after all that we shared? Really Caleb, how?" she asked as her eyes began to sting from the tears that were now welling up. She hated how he was able to get so much emotion from her. *He doesn't even deserve the conversation that I'm giving him*, she thought.

"C'mon Cami, don't you think it's about time that you hear me out? I didn't—"

"Forget it! I don't want to hear anything else that you have to say." She ended the conversation by getting into her car, slamming the door and speeding out of the parking lot.

"Ugh! He just makes me so sick! What in the world is he doing here anyway? How could he have ended up in the same place as Rico? This can't be real." *Oh but it is,* she thought. "I know Rico is going to ask about this again. I don't know what to tell him or even how to tell him the full story," she said to herself as she drove off. At this point, she was becoming convinced that she didn't quite know the entire story. *Am I really being unreasonable,* she questioned.

The ringing and vibration of her phone interrupted her monologue.

"Girl," Kensi spoke into the receiver, dragging the word out. "What happened? I couldn't wait until later, I need the deets now," Kensi said. Raegan could hear the excitement in her voice.

"Where are you and how did you know that I wasn't still talking to him?" Raegan said, still a little flustered.

"You're forgetting one thing Rae…I know you! You weren't going to talk to him for too long and probably wouldn't have talked to him at all if I didn't encourage you," Kensi said laughing.

"Anyway," Raegan said rolling her eyes, "We need to sit down for this. Let's meet up."

"I was actually heading to the new coffee shop west of the theater district to catch up on some work before my training next week. Meet me there. I'm approaching now."

"That sounds good. I hear they have great lattes. I'm heading your way now. Give me about fifteen minutes," Raegan said as she ended the call. She was still visibly shaken from her recent interaction with Caleb. It took the remainder of the car ride for her to calm down.

CHAPTER 17

∞

Kensi pulled up to the coffee shop and went inside. She could see the blinking signage hanging in the window, *Try our new caramel lattes.* She grabbed cozy booth seats for herself and Raegan and decided to snoop around on the internet to see what Caleb was now up to, or at least what he allowed the world to know through Facebook. *Hmmmm,* she thought. *Still single. Handsome.* She wished she could have witnessed the reunion between Raegan and Caleb, at most just to see Raegan's face when she first saw him. Just as she was clicking through his profile and pictures, Raegan walked in.

Without wasting any time, Kensi asked, "What happened with Caleb and why are you looking like that?!" Her eyes bright, she leaned forward in her chair and motioned for Raegan to sit down.

"Why?" Raegan questioned in her most dramatic tone of voice, throwing her hands in the air imitating a terrible actor.

"Skim the dramatics. Tell me what happened," Kensi pushed.

"Typical pretty boy Caleb, wanting to get his way with me, flashing his pretty teeth and giving me puppy dog eyes," Raegan began. She inwardly swooned at the sight of him. He was more handsome than she remembered. "He went on with some noise about wanting me and that I should listen to him to at least get the truth about that dreadful night." Raegan continued on without giving her friend a chance to speak because she knew what she would say. "I mean, really! It's been so long and so much has changed since then. I mean, what are the chances of me even seeing him today?" Raegan sighed and paused for a moment. "Part of me wants to talk about it now so that I can get some closure, but it really wouldn't change anything." *At least I don't think.*

A handsome waiter interrupted them. "Here are your two caramel lattes," he said cheerily, showing a bright white smile. Kensi had ordered their drinks while she waited for Raegan to arrive.

"Thank you," they said in unison.

"Thanks Kensi. This is my favorite cup of hot coffee, caramel latte. A sip of this yummy goodness is just what I needed," she said. She took a sip while peering over her cup only to find Kensi's hazel brown eyes staring at her.

"What?" Rae asked, confused.

"You are afraid of what Caleb will say, aren't you? What if nothing happened? You're going to start feeling like you need to make a decision now and choose between Caleb and Rico...No one is asking you to make a decision about this now, nor do we know that you will ever need to. You always think way too far in advance, putting too much pressure on yourself. I think the real problem is that you still have feelings for Caleb and you're afraid to admit it or confront those feelings," Kensi said as she shot an imaginary ball into a basket as if scoring in a basketball game.

"You don't have to say anything but I know I'm right on point again," Kensi said, smiling.

"Ugh, you make me sick too!" Raegan said laughing. "Why am I even considering this if I love Rico so much? I mean, it was just last night that I was sitting around laughing and talking with you guys telling you how much I like him."

Quickly interrupting Raegan, Kensi added, "and also voicing your uncertainty." Kensi wanted to see Raegan with Caleb.

"Yeah, *but* he's still my beau and Caleb just had to come messing that up."

"How is he messing that up? Did you leave something out of that half-story you just told me? Don't think I missed how you left out tons of details. Classic Rae," Kensi said, shaking her head in disapproval.

"What details did I leave out? The interaction was short. He stated he wanted *me,* but I still don't know what he meant by that. He then stated that I should hear him out about that little incident that tore our relationship apart back in college. I said no, doesn't matter and left. That was it" Raegan said, summing up her encounter with Caleb.

"Well, it is obvious that it does matter, or else you wouldn't be sitting here discussing it with me. By the way, what does Rico have to say about this?" Kensi paused, waiting for Raegan's response. "Wait, does he even know *who* Caleb is?" she said laughing. "Poor fella. He doesn't even know what he is now up against."

"I really don't see the amusement and no, he doesn't know the full story. I didn't want to talk about it." The truth is that Raegan was now trying to sort through everything herself. Raegan knew that Rico was going to want to know more. *There is no way that he is going to let this go under the radar. He asks too many questions,* questions that she herself didn't have answers to. "Do you think I came up in their conversation?" Raegan wondered.

"Rae, why are you asking questions that you already know the answer to? Of course you came up! Rico is probably trying to be slick and get any information out of the guy that he can bring up again in conversation with you!" Taking a sip of her latte, she continued. "Why didn't you just tell Rico that Caleb *was* the one? He can't do anything about that. It's all in the past," she said using air quotes again. "At least for now," she said, smiling.

Kensi was right. Raegan secretly desired to see Caleb again, although she didn't know how she would deal with it. Now that they'd seen each other again, there was no way that things could stay the way they had been between them. Silence. Tension. Unforgiveness. At least all on Raegan's part. Caleb on the other hand had been waiting for such a moment. A chance where he could reconnect with the love of his life.

"So does that mean you're going to get the scoop on Caleb for me?" Raegan asked. She was curious about what he had been up to, and if she knew Kensi, she was probably already ahead of her.

"I didn't know you cared so much," Kensi teased.

"Not really. But I'm all grown up now; I can handle it." Raegan noticed the shift in her friend's face as she flipped her laptop open again. "What is it? Do you know something that I don't know?" She paused and turned to look her friend in the eye.

"Well," Kensi stated emphatically, "I may know a little something. And before you say anything, I never said a word to you about it because you didn't want to hear anything remotely having to deal with Caleb. You know how you are…" Raegan always tuned anyone out whenever they would mention his name. "Plus, I'm not entirely sure how much of it is true so I didn't want to bring it up. I assumed that you two would eventually work it out."

"I'm listening now." Raegan sat with her arms folded, ears perked up. She wanted to know everything that Kensi even *thought* she knew about that night. Even though it took her a decade to listen, she was ready now.

Kensi recalled what she knew about that night. Raegan stopped by Caleb's frat party looking for him. One of his frat brothers told her that he was in the room with someone else, a woman. Angry, Raegan went to the door, attempted to open it and it was locked. Upset, she stormed out of the frat house, walking back to her car. Moments later, Caleb came running out of the house behind her and she turned around and slapped him without even giving him a chance to speak. That was exactly how Raegan remembered that night.

Raegan thought there was no reason to hear what he had to say after he was locked in the bedroom with someone else. What could he have said that would change anything?

"How do you even know that it was Caleb in the room? Did you actually see him?" Kensi questioned.

Raegan pondered Kensi's question. With all of the time that had passed, Raegan never even considered that Caleb wasn't the one in the room. She never even thought to verify that it was him. She honestly didn't know who was in the room. In fact, the mere thought of it being Caleb sent her into a rage. It was enough that they struggled with purity and the thought of him sharing what they shared with someone else was just too much for her to even think about. That type of hurt was unforgivable in her mind.

Kensi took Raegan's silence as the answer to her question. "So you ran off and threw your entire relationship away without any actual proof?" Kensi asked, confused. They had never really discussed the subject until now because Raegan had always been so stubborn.

"Well, that doesn't really change anything. Why would anyone say that he was in the room if he wasn't?" Raegan defended, justifying ending her relationship with him. At that time, she felt like any reasonable person would have done the same thing.

"Girl, the person who told you that was probably drunk and had no idea what their own name was, let alone who was where." Kensi was making sense. Raegan knew how wild those fraternity parties could be, but in her mind, the Caleb she knew wouldn't have allowed anyone to even think that he was doing such a thing.

"What if what you're suggesting is true? I'm too embarrassed to even admit my part in being wrong in all of this," she said, leaning back in the booth and resting her hands on her forehead. "I guess I do need to hear his side of the story." *But what about Rico?* Raegan felt a knot in the pit of her stomach. What would it mean if Caleb never cheated? They couldn't just pick up where they were before the break-up because so many things had changed. But Caleb was the one she thought she would marry.

"You're going to need to find out though, honey. No one is saying that you have to do it today, although I'd like to know today." She winked. "Besides, he's in town and I'm in town. I'd rather receive the juicy details of this reunion in person," Kensi said, slightly joking. "I'm laughing but I am so serious. So what *are* you going to do?"

"Like you just said, I don't have to do anything today. I think I need to sleep on it."

"How much longer is he here again?"

"I don't know. I didn't ask, remember?"

"Well, how long is his fraternity's convention?"

"A few more days, I guess," Raegan said as if she was unsure. Because of her involvement with Rico, she knew how long the convention was scheduled go on.

After finishing off their second cups of lattes and friendly chatter, Raegan decided to go home and rest. She had a late night with her friends and one heck of a day. She encouraged Kensi to stay with her so they could attend church together the next morning. Having Kensi around also gave her an excuse not to spend too much time talking to Rico and explaining the whole Caleb situation. All of that would just have to wait.

CHAPTER 18

∞

Kensi joined Raegan at church as promised. The pastor preached about forgiveness.

"Matthew 6:14-15 says, 'For if you forgive other people when they sin against you, your heavenly Father will also forgive you. But if you do not forgive others their sins, your Father will not forgive your sins,'" the Pastor said as he began his sermon.

Raegan felt heat rising on the back of her neck after hearing the scripture reference. She immediately felt convicted because of the grudge and bad feelings she held against Caleb for wronging her. All she could think about during the rest of the sermon was the whole ordeal involving Caleb. She actually missed most of the message because her mind wandered back and forth between whether or not she should call him to hear his side of the story. It had been so long, she didn't know what to expect or how his words would change things. *What about Rico?* She continued to wonder. She really liked him but she had doubts. But who didn't have doubts? Her thoughts were interrupted by Kensi nudging her in the side.

"Pass me an offering envelope," Kensi whispered.

"Oh, sorry." Raegan didn't realize that the usher had his hand extended towards her to pass the envelope over to Kensi. Where had she been? The service was ending. "Here you go. Did you take good notes?" Raegan asked.

"Of course I did. From the looks of things, you're going to need them because your page is empty," Kensi said, tapping Raegan's notebook.

Raegan glanced down to see that she'd only written today's date, Scripture reference, subject and the pastor's first point. "I'm glad you did. I will copy your notes later," Raegan said, trying to silence the thoughts that continued to erupt in her mind.

When service ended, Raegan and Kensi went out to brunch to chat some more before Kensi had to check into her hotel and begin preparing for her work week. During brunch, Kensi encouraged Raegan to call Caleb before he left town. "You're going to regret it if you don't," Kensi said to her one final time before leaving.

When Raegan returned home from brunch, Kensi's words rang in her ears along with the words from today's sermon. Kensi reminded her that she would regret not talking to Caleb and the last thing she needed right now was more regrets. She took her church clothes off, slipped on her yoga pants and tank top and reclined in her chair. She pulled out her phone and began to dial Caleb's number. After all of those years, she still had his number memorized. Before she could complete the number, she hung up and took a few deep breaths. She had to prepare herself to hear his voice and for what he might say.

"All right, just breathe. You have nothing to be afraid of. This is just a conversation. You are only calling to get the facts. Nothing more. Nothing less," Raegan spoke to herself, trying to calm her nerves. "I can't believe I'm so nervous and shaking. Why am I being this silly?" she questioned.

Getting her nerves together, she quickly dialed his number and somewhat hoped that his voicemail would pick up. Before she could finish the thought, he answered.

"Cami." She could hear his smile as his deep familiar voice spoke her name.

"Hey, Caleb. Listen…I thought a little about what you were trying to say to me in the parking lot yesterday; I'm ready to hear what you have to say." There, she said it. *That wasn't so bad*, she thought to herself, letting out a long sigh as she pulled the phone away from her mouth so that he wouldn't hear it.

Whatever his response, she didn't hear him..

"I'm sorry, I missed that. What did you say?"

"I said that I would much rather talk to you about it in person. I need to see your face and I need you to see mine," Caleb said, not wanting to miss this opportunity. The fraternity events would have to wait. Now that he had laid eyes on her again, his business with her was way more important.

"Caleb, why can't we just talk about this on the phone?" she whined. She knew that her eyes would give her away and Caleb knew that as well. She needed time to process whatever he would tell her, and she didn't want him to be able to read her expressions. But deep down, she really wanted to see him.

"No…I think we need to have this conversation in person. Besides, I'm only in town for a few more days." He chose not to reveal to her that he was also in town looking for a place to live because his company was sending him there to lead their new business unit.

"Okay, fine. Where do you want to meet?" She relented.

"Let's grab dessert. I know how you love ice cream. Is there a Blue Bells around?"

"Yes Caleb, but that's too far away from me. Let's just meet at Char. They have the greatest dessert ever! I love it," Raegan said. Her mouth watered just thinking about her favorite dessert, only served at Char.

"That's cool, too. Any place is fine as long as it's not over the phone," he said. She should have known that one phone call was not going to be sufficient, especially after all of this time. "Text me the address so that I can put it into my GPS."

"Texting now." Raegan figured that she could meet up with him and get back home in time to relax before work tomorrow. She also knew that Rico was attending one of his fraternity events tonight and she wouldn't have to worry about seeing him or explaining where she was or whose company she was keeping.

Raegan slipped out of her lounge clothes and rummaged through her closet to find something cute, yet simple. She didn't want him to think that she was dressing up for him or that she put *too* much effort into her wardrobe. She settled on a purple, casual, long sleeved wrap dress and coordinating flats. She showered and touched up her soft curls before heading out of the door. As she curled her hair, she reminded herself to stay calm and just listen. *Don't show any emotion.* After her pep talk and one final primp, she felt confident enough to face the situation head on.

CHAPTER 19

∞

Raegan's drive to the restaurant felt like an eternity although the ride was smooth with light traffic and few red lights. She wasn't breathing normally and she didn't realize it until she exhaled and let out a long breath of air upon arriving at the restaurant. The tension she felt was evidenced by her sore back. *Get a grip,* she coaxed herself.

While looking for a parking space, she saw that Caleb was already there, punctual just like she remembered. He stood in front of the glass revolving doors at the entrance, near valet parking, waiting to escort her into the building. Parking her car, she exhaled slowly and deeply, gathered her composure, got out of the car and walked towards the entrance.

Caleb's eyes immediately captured hers as she neared him. As she held his gaze, his smooth voice began to echo in her ear. "Cami, thanks for meeting me," he said as he grabbed her hand, quickly brought it to his mouth and caressed it with his lips. The move startled Raegan but she was pleased nonetheless. *Here we go,* she thought.

"You're welcome," was all she could muster.

He extended his left hand toward the door, gesturing that she should enter first. He was always a gentleman. That was one of the things that she liked about him. Raegan sauntered past him, being careful not to sway her hips too much or too little. She wanted to make sure that he didn't think that she was trying to impress him.

He watched her as she walked in front of him, admiring her class and elegance. He missed her so much and hoped that tonight he would get a chance to make things right between them.

"Welcome to Char! Will it just be the two of you?" the hostess asked.

"Yes," they responded in unison.

The hostess grabbed two menus and requested that they follow her to an empty booth in the rear of the restaurant.

"I hope this works okay for you two. Please enjoy your evening here at Char," the hostess said with a smile as she placed their menus on the table, whipped her long blonde hair over her shoulder and walked away.

Raegan was grateful for the seating in the rear of the restaurant because she had a pretty good view of the entire place, including the entrance and exit doors. She didn't think Rico would show up there but just in case he did, she would spot him long before he would see her. He should be with his fraternity brothers at the convention anyway.

Waiting for Raegan to slide into the booth, Caleb remained standing until she was comfortably sitting. After she sat down, he began thanking her again for meeting him and immediately picked up the conversation where they left off on the telephone.

"Cami, it is so good to see you," he said again, flashing his bright white smile that showed his slightly crooked bottom tooth. "You know, after all that's happened between us, I never thought that we would ever sit down like this again. But that didn't stop me from hoping and praying it would happen. I appreciate you giving me the benefit of the doubt, even if it has been a hundred years," He said. His gaze remained locked on hers.

Fiddling with the black cloth napkin in her lap, she smiled and remained quiet, motioning with her head for him to continue. She didn't want to waste any time. Far too much time had already passed, and after talking things over with Kensi she was quite interested to hear what he had to say now.

"First of all, I never cheated on you. When you came to the frat house that night, I was not in the bedroom with anyone. In fact, I wasn't locked up in that bedroom at all. I was in the bathroom, sick from either the alcohol or something that I had eaten earlier that day or possibly a combination of both. When I came out of the bathroom, one of my brothers told me that you had just left. When I heard that, I came running out of the house to find you, and that's when I called your name and you turned around to slap me. You didn't give me a chance to say anything. I had no idea what happened or what even warranted that reaction from you. It wasn't until later that I found out that Michael was locked up in the room with Stacy and you thought that it was me," Caleb said, elbows bent on the table, shaking his head in confusion. Revisiting that night brought back intense feelings. He was visibly agitated.

Interrupting him, she said, "Well, I didn't just pull that thought out of thin air. Kendrick was the one who mentioned it when I came inside looking for you."

"How could you listen to him? I'm sure he was pretty drunk and I think we previously established that he had a thing for you anyway. He would do anything to pull us apart. Looks like he succeeded," Caleb stated. The disappointment was clearly written over his face.

"How was I to know, Caleb?" Raegan defended herself. The thought never crossed her mind that someone would lie to her like that.

"You weren't, but you didn't try to find out the truth either. I was really upset at the thought that you would think I could do something like that to you and even more upset that you called our relationship off without giving me a chance to explain." Caleb grew more frustrated as he continued to talk. "I thought we had a pretty decent relationship, so I was very confused by everything that transpired. I mean, I knew I must have missed something and that you had to have been upset about something else. Tell me Cami, why would you throw our relationship away without even talking to me? I thought we agreed that we would always talk to each other. I don't want to hear that you were young, we were kids or any other excuse you can come up with. Give me the real reason," he demanded, now leaning in closer to her.

Raegan could see his growing frustration because he no longer wore a smile. Confusion and hurt were all over his face. If she didn't know any better, she could have sworn that his eyes were a tad bit watery as well.

"You know Caleb, I can't really explain myself. I can tell you that I was livid when I heard that you were locked in the room with Stacy. I went to that bedroom and the door was locked. I banged on the door, screaming your name and you didn't come open the door! I even stood there for a few minutes waiting for you to come out. All I could hear were sounds of ecstasy and what sounded like a headboard bumping up against a wall. Can you imagine what I felt like in that moment? A fool, Caleb! I felt so humiliated, betrayed and angry! When you walked out of that house, I wanted to give you much more than a slap." Tears were now streaming down her face because she could no longer contain her emotion and her voice had become slightly elevated. Caleb scooted closer to her and began to hold her, rubbing her shoulders.

"How could we both have been so stupid? We've lost so many years because of that misunderstanding," Caleb said slowly, thinking out loud, wondering what they would do next. "What does this mean for us Cami?"

"I honestly don't know." And she didn't. How was she to know that he was telling her the truth? She wanted to believe him. She actually needed to believe him. She once loved him so much, and if she was being honest with herself, part of her still had some feelings for him. *But then there's Rico,* a small voice echoed in her mind.

"Can we at least start by being friends again?" he asked as he scooted back to his place setting. He knew she was with Rico, but he now had every intention of winning her back. There was no way he was going to let her go this time. There was one thing that he and Raegan had that she and Rico didn't, and that was history, a very good one except for that sour moment that tore them apart.

"Yes, why not? We deserve that much, don't we?" she said smiling and dabbing her eyes with the napkin that she had wrinkled up from anxiety. It was a good thing that she didn't wear makeup tonight because her face would be a mess.

"I hate to bring up old stuff, so after tonight, can we leave the past in the past?" he asked before he began asking questions about way back when.

"Agreed," Raegan nodded.

"Why didn't you confront me if you thought that I slept with someone else?" he asked, still trying to see things from Raegan's point of view.

"I figured there was nothing that you could have said to make things better, especially after what I thought I witnessed."

"Okay, but why didn't you respond to any of my letters or messages," he pressed, looking for answers to questions that he'd asked himself for years.

"Same answer as before," she stated laughing. "I'm sorry but I didn't think we needed to communicate at all after that night."

"You didn't think that our love was worth saving?" he asked softly, his gaze intense.

"I felt like you had thrown it all away and besides, I was only twenty and we weren't married. I didn't feel the need to save anything or work it out with you. You had made your choice, or so I thought," Raegan said, defending her actions.

"And so you gave up on us." Caleb wondered if she ever really loved him like she said she did.

"And so did you!" she said as she sipped her glass of water.

"I know not to ever cross you, because there would be no coming back," Caleb said, relieved that he was getting another chance with her.

"You're right. I just feel like this: If you didn't care enough to stay, why should I care enough to try to keep you or work things out with you? I'd much rather be alone."

Interrupting their conversation, the waitress stopped by their table to take their orders.

"We'll just be having dessert tonight. Cami, did you change your mind or do you still only want dessert?" he asked, directing the waitress to her.

"Yes, only dessert and I'll take the pecan caramel butter crunch please," she said smiling and handing the waitress the menu. That was her favorite dessert and she could not wait to take pleasure in the delectable delight that was topped with caramel and homemade vanilla ice cream. She knew she would probably need extra time in the gym to make up for eating it, but in her eyes it was well worth that extra mile or two on the treadmill.

"I'll just have an apple pie," Caleb said as he handed the waitress his menu and mouthed to Raegan, "and eat some of your dessert too."

"Still greedy, huh?" she said laughing. She was happy that they were going to work on becoming friends again. They had such great times together. She dared not compare but he was actually better company than Rico. Oh, Rico! *How am I going to explain this to him*, she silently questioned herself. *Do I even have to explain it at all*? So many questions. So few answers.

CHAPTER 20

∞

After Raegan and Caleb's long overdue talk, they chatted as if no time had passed. It felt natural. Comfortable.

"So, tell me about your work. How is that going? What is it you do again?" Raegan asked, taking a sip of water.

"I'm an architectural designer, where my focus is commercial designing and construction. I love designing plans for our clients; and it's really rewarding to see their excitement when they review what I've come up with." Seeing that he had her interest, he continued, "In other good news, I recently finished my Master of Architecture degree, so I am currently exploring career advancement opportunities. Sometime in the future, though, I may consider starting my own architectural firm." Smiling and staring intently into her eyes, he said in a much lower voice, "I may need to hire you to help with recruiting interns and staff for my business."

"As long as I can work remotely and you're willing to pay the big bucks, count me in," she said, playing along with him. "But that's great Caleb. It sounds like you're doing quite well career wise. I'm happy for you. How is your family?" She asked, posed with her chin resting in her palm, fully engrossed in the conversation.

Both of their families lived in Florida. Her family lived in Jacksonville, his in Tampa. While they were dating, they visited both families during the holidays.

"My mom is doing well. She retired last year and now spends most of her time taking care of Dad. He took an early retirement after getting hurt at work. He gets around pretty well with the leg injury but still needs assistance. My sister had twins last year, so Mom helps out a lot with the babies as well."

"Wow, last year seemed to be a pretty big year for your family, huh?"

"Yes! My baby brother John graduated from FAMU last year! Can you believe it?"

"My goodness, it has been so long! The last time I saw him, I think he was just entering middle school. Time flies that that," she said, snapping her fingers.

"You're right about that Cami, but it looks like you've been taking advantage of all the time you have—MBA, house, excelling at work and a new boyfriend."

She didn't miss the slight saltiness in his tone when he mentioned her relationship with Rico. "Yes, I have to admit that things are going well in my life right now." *And you had to come along and try to make things all difficult for me,* she thought to herself. "Rico seems like a nice guy and we've been having a really good time together. You should have gotten some sort of glimpse into his character; you just broke bread with him."

"I did and he's okay. You can definitely do better," he said, winking and curling his lips into a smile. Caleb thought of himself as the much better choice—the right choice for Raegan. He just hoped that it didn't take Raegan very long to figure that out as well.

"I'll be the judge of that; I'd like to see where things go with him. He's sweet." At this point, she felt she owed it to herself to see how things would work out with Rico since she had given herself to him.

"Yeah, that's what you think. I'm a guy and I can tell you right now that something is off about him. I can't quite put my finger on it, but something just doesn't sit well with me," he said, shaking his head as if in deep thought.

"Where did this inkling of a feeling come from? Was it something that he said or did?" Raegan sometimes felt like something was a little off with Rico but she always shook the feeling off. Since Caleb thought that something may be wrong, she wanted to know what he thought, although she knew that he was biased because he liked her.

Turning his nose up, he stated, "I just don't know about him Cami. I've always wanted the best for you, even when you didn't want me, so I will just warn you to keep your eyes open and not to get caught up in all of his *sweetness*. Can you promise me that? Just be careful."

"You are making it sound so gloomy and doomy. What did he say or do that has you warning me? Just tell me. I can handle it. I'm a big girl, remember?"

"I just get the feeling that he's hiding something. How long have you known him?"

"Not very long. Just a few months actually."

"Has he already professed his love for you and you him?" He asked mainly because he was trying to gauge how deeply involved Raegan had gotten with Rico and how much he would have to do to win her over again.

"Wait, where's our dessert?" she asked, trying to distract Caleb. It was awkward discussing her relationship with Rico.

"I don't know. It has been quite a while and it's not even crowded. I'll get the waitress' attention." Just as he was motioning to the waitress to come to the table, someone from the kitchen was walking toward their table with the large serving tray on his shoulder.

"Oh, wait, I think that may be ours," Raegan said hopefully.

The waiter approached the booth and spoke as if he'd been eating sweets all day. He was very spirited. "Hello! I have a pecan caramel crunch and an apple pie." They both reached for their dishes as Raegan prepared to dig in.

"Hold on dear, let's take a quick second to pray," he said as he extended his hands toward hers. "I know it's only dessert but I'm still thankful. *God has finally answered my prayers and brought you back into my life,* he thought.

There he goes, she thought. "I won't turn down prayer but be sure to make it quick," she said batting her eyes. Her body immediately grew warm at the touch of his hands, coupled with her heart skipping a few beats.

Caleb prayed for their desserts, the two of them, and traveling grace for the two of them as they returned home.

"Amen," they stated in unison.

"Thanks Caleb."

"No problem. You never answered my question either," he reminded her.

"What question is that?" she asked with a puzzled look on her face. She knew exactly what question he was referring to, but she had hoped he would have moved on by now.

"I asked you if Rico has professed his love for you and if you've professed your love for him," Caleb stated, taking a bite of his dessert.

"Yeah…but I don't want to talk about that. We haven't talked to each other in years; there are so many other things we can talk about," she said, hoping to change the subject again.

Raegan successfully diverted Caleb's attention to other things as they ate dessert. They talked more about their families, careers, friends and church involvement. Raegan was happy that she had decided to see him again. She had almost forgotten how comfortable she was around him and how much she enjoyed his company. Luckily for her, he was leaving in a few days; otherwise he would truly make things complicated for her. After their dessert, Caleb took care of the check and they walked out of the restaurant.

"Where did you park your car?" he asked opening the door so that she could walk out first. "I'll walk with you."

"I'm straight ahead about two rows down," Raegan said, pointing in the direction of her car.

As they walked, Caleb broke the silence. "It was really great sitting down talking with you again Cami. You probably don't want to hear this but I do miss you," he said sincerely. "Hopefully we can catch up again soon."

"I enjoyed talking with you again, too. Although it took forever, thanks for taking the time to explain things to me. I'm glad that we can be friends again. Forgive me for being so stubborn," she said, stopping when they made it to her car.

She turned and gazed into his eyes for a moment. Glad that he was more forgiving than she would have been. She had to admit that she missed him too. Everything about him. Her gaze shifted to his hands as he reached out to rub her arms. His then grabbed both of her hands.

"I know the position you thought I put you into, but all of that is behind us now. Let's just move on, okay?" he said as he motioned to hug her. She honored his request and gave him a hug, relishing in the smell of his cologne. She unlocked her car and Caleb opened the door for her, and watched as she revved up the engine and drove away. He had much hope that things were finally turning around for him in the relationship department and that he had a great chance of winning her back. It would just take a little time. It didn't matter how long because he was up to the challenge.

CHAPTER 21

∞

The four friends had brunch and then parted ways as Kensi returned home and Tammy left for a business trip to Boston. When she landed in Boston, she remembered that the Celtics had a home game that she planned to attend. She figured it would be a great way to entertain a client and get what she wanted too–to see Josh. They spoke on the phone from time to time but she couldn't remember the last time she saw his face. It had been so long.

She had to find something suitable to wear. She wondered if she could find something with his jersey number on it. Of course, that would do nothing but boost his ego. On her way to baggage claim, she stopped in one of the airport's gift shops to see if she could find a cute tee to sport to the game in a few days. As she browsed the shop, she noticed pictures of him and his teammates plastered everywhere. She couldn't escape him in this city even if she wanted to. Flipping through the racks, she came across a fitted bling tee with his jersey number on the chest.

"Oh, this is absolutely perfect and it's just my size. I will slip on a pair of my skinny jeans with this and his heart is going to turn flips!" she whispered to herself while holding the shirt up to her chest, looking in a mirror.

The gift shop was quite fancy for an airport store, she thought. She picked up a package of pistachio nuts along with her shirt, paid for her purchases and headed to baggage claim.

Tammy hailed a taxi to the hotel instead of renting a car. She didn't have any friends to visit in Boston so much of her trip would be strictly business. When she arrived at the hotel and checked in her room, she was happy to see that her accommodations were very nice. She was staying in the Ritz Carlton and the pillows on that bed were cause for anyone to miss the alarm clock in the morning. She quickly settled in and ordered room service.

"Everything looks so good!" she exclaimed, talking to the menu. "What am I going to get? No salad today. Let's go with this six ounce steak, twice baked mashed potatoes, broccoli and a fruit tray," she said aloud before calling room service to place her order.

After placing her order, she took a shower, washed her hair and relaxed in one of those comfy robes and flicked through the television channels to find a great movie. She was just getting comfortable when her food arrived. The steak was medium well just as she liked it and those buttery potatoes were to die for, loaded with all of the ingredients that she liked. The broccoli was steamed perfectly and the fruit looked as if it was freshly picked from a farmer's market. She didn't waste any time tearing into the food. This was her first time all day eating a full meal and she was not going to let it go to waste. Once finished, she set the tray outside of her door and curled back up into bed.

It felt good to relax without all the noise and commotion. She enjoyed being in hotels from time to time. She didn't have to clean or cook; she just had to *be*. After relaxing for a while, she prepared for her workweek. She reviewed her presentations and organized her documents for the many meetings scheduled throughout the week.

With all of the work that needed to be done, her week went by quickly, but maybe not as quickly as she had hoped. She was anxious about going to the game for many reasons. She was taking one of their top clients to the game. This was an opportunity for her to win the client over and renew their contract. If all went well, she could definitely see a promotion in her future. In addition to that, she hoped that the client was a fan of Josh because that would work well in her favor. She could introduce them. After all, she and the client would be sitting on the floor. Those were expensive seats, but her firm would spare no expense to keep this client. This was one of their biggest clients, so spending a few thousand bucks was no big deal at all.

It was finally Wednesday, the day of the game. Her presentations went smoothly at work that day and she made sure she spent time taking the client to lunch and answering all of his questions. She was only in town one and a half more days before returning to Houston, so she had to make sure she made a lasting impression.

"Tammy, is everything all set for the game tonight? You know I'm a huge fan of the Boston Celtics," Gary asked.

"Sure thing, Gary," Tammy said. Gary was a handsome guy. He reminded her of Blair Underwood. He was clean shaven and always neatly dressed. From what she could see, he seemed to be in great shape.

"Great, I will send a car to pick you up. Just leave the address to your hotel with the receptionist on your way out today." Usually, Tammy's company provided transportation for their clients but Gary insisted that she get picked up.

"You're so kind, thank you. I really appreciate that. I like basketball myself, so I'm looking forward to the game as well," Tammy said.

"Awesome, I will see you then," Gary said as he exited the conference room. He had a few more meetings that afternoon, so Tammy spent some time meeting with the managers in the local office.

After her meetings, she headed back to her hotel to get changed for the game. She retouched her makeup and curled her hair. She made sure everything was in place for tonight. She couldn't risk Joshua seeing her off her game.

Tammy called Raegan for a pep talk. She knew she was going to hear words from Raegan, because she hadn't told Raegan that she was going to Boston or that she was planning to see Joshua while she was there.

She picked up the phone to dial her friend, hoping that she would answer.

"Tammy, what's up? How's your trip going?" Raegan sang into the phone.

"Raegan," she said as soon as Raegan answered the phone. "It's your turn to boost me up. I'm in Boston and I'm heading to a basketball game!" Tammy paused for a second because she knew Raegan was about to fuss.

"Now hold on a minute…I think I'm missing a ton of information here. I need to know the full story before I do any boosting," she said laughing. This sounded as if it was going to be good. Raegan had just finished the dishes and curled up in front of the fireplace with her favorite blanket. She didn't need the television because she had a feeling she was going to get all the entertainment she needed in the next few minutes. She somehow thought that Tammy would be in New York, not Boston.

"You're not missing anything. I had to come to Boston for work this week. I'm entertaining a client tonight by taking him to the game."

"You're not fooling me one bit. You know that I know that you have control over where and how you entertain clients. You planned this. You want to see Joshua, don't you? It's about time," Raegan said, answering her own question.

"See…you're caught up; I need a pep talk. I'm a little on edge," Tammy said, pacing back and forth in her hotel room.

"If you're already headed to a game, I don't think you need me to boost you up. You have all the power you need girlfriend!"

"Seriously Raegan, I need to be ready when I see him. We're going to be sitting on the floor, so he will see us," Tammy said, chewing her bottom lip as she continued pacing the floor.

"Here's an idea. Use the client as an excuse, as you're already doing. Stay behind after the game to introduce your client to Joshua. Is the client a big fan?"

"Yeah."

"Well, there you go. You will score big points on both sides. The client will be excited that he's gotten a chance to meet a player and Joshua will be happy that you came to see him. No matter what you tell him, he will think that everything is for him anyway, right?"

"Yeah, you're right about that," Tammy paused mid step. She was confident that her plan was solid as she considered Raegan's conclusion.

"Boost accomplished," Raegan said laughing. "Just have a good time and be sure to call me afterwards. Well, I guess that will be tomorrow because I know that Josh isn't going to let you just walk away after the introduction. You'll probably be seeing him tonight, so call me as soon as you get a chance. I want all the deets! Just like I gave you."

"Of course! You may receive a text or two so hug that phone like it's your undies," Tammy said laughing.

"Only you would say something like that," Raegan said through giggles. "Have fun and call me later."

"All right, bye," Tammy said, ending the call.

CHAPTER 22

∞

As Raegan sat in her office on Wednesday, typing away at her computer preparing reports, a tap on the half-opened door interrupted her.

"Raegan, please come to my office. I'm ready to discuss your goals for the next fiscal year and review your performance," Marie said and walked away. Marie was her immediate manager as well as a mentor. She made sure that Raegan was aware of any training opportunities or voluntary assignments that would enhance her performance on the job. She really liked Raegan and wanted to see her excel.

"Okay, thanks," Raegan said, as she grabbed her notepad and pen. She was so busy that she'd almost forgotten about her meeting with Marie today. On the way, Raegan peeped into Michelle's office.

"Hey! I'm about to have my performance review but will try to stop and chat with you for a few moments when we're done. That is, if you're not being superwoman in here." She smiled at her friend and walked away, not giving her a chance to respond.

Raegan walked down the hall to Marie's office, slightly nervous, but excited about their discussion. She couldn't wait to share her goals, but she was feeling a little anxious about her review. She had no idea what feedback she would get from other team members. As part of her performance evaluation, Raegan also had a peer review. She was on the fast track to senior management, so it was very important that her peers thought of her as a leader and motivator.

Although she did a great job, she sometimes felt as if the higher-ups thought that she wasn't doing her best. However, she worked additional hours and took on more challenging assignments to prove that she was serious about her career and upward mobility.

When she entered Marie's office, Marie motioned for her to close the door and take a seat in front of her desk. She rubbed her hands down the front of her green tweed blazer as if to straighten it out and sat down in the comfy leather seat, crossing her legs at the ankles.

"Raegan, as always, you've been doing such a great job. Steve and Mike have both been paying attention to your work and they feel like you're ready to take on management-related tasks. How do you feel about this?

More work could possibly mean later nights at the office," Marie informed her, as if she wanted her to think carefully about her response. She peered over her glasses waiting for Raegan's response.

"I'm sure it's nothing that I can't handle," Raegan said confidently. She would not allow a few extra hours to keep her away from her goals. She was ready to become manager. Based on her calculations, if she received her promotion this year, she could easily get a senior management position in three years.

"I am not supposed to tell you this yet, but once your performance review is finalized and you're evaluated on these new assignments, Steve is going to promote you to a level one manager. That means that you're going to start leading recruiting efforts in the east region by preparing strategies and plans on what we can do to bring in the greatest talent."

"Wow! That is great news! Hopefully that won't be too long from now. I'm so excited!" Raegan squealed.

"I knew that would put a sparkle into your eyes," Marie said. And it did. They continued to discuss Raegan's performance, her goals and how she would transition into her newly assigned duties. The additional work was to help her become acclimated in her new position. She wished that she could share the news with Michelle, but since it was not official yet, she would have to wait. Besides, Michelle had yet to have her performance review so Raegan didn't want to share the news with her until Michelle received news about what was next for her.

One and a half hours later, Raegan's meeting with Marie was over and Raegan went back to her office. It took everything in her not to run down the hall in her four-inch Steve Madden pumps, screaming for joy. Well, if she couldn't tell Michelle the good news, she would just share it with someone else.

"Mommy!" she said with much enthusiasm. "How are you? What are you doing? Guess what?"

"Hey baby! Slow down. How are you doing, sweetheart? It's so good to hear your voice," Raegan's mother said.

"Thanks Mommy. I have some great news to share with you," Raegan said, as she took one quick spin in her leather chair.

"Is it about a boy or work?" Her mother questioned.

"Mom-ma!" she said whining. "It's not always about a guy. It is about work though. I can't say this too loud so I'm going to whisper into the phone. Pay attention please." Her mom was caring for her dad, and being hard of hearing must have been one of his undiagnosed issues because the television volume was always on 100. "Wait, Mommy, please ask Daddy to turn the TV down. It sounds like it's sitting right here in my office."

"Frank, please turn the TV down. My baby is on the phone trying to whisper something to me. I don't know why she just won't go outside to talk on the phone like regular people."

Raegan didn't miss the slug her mother had shot at her, but she just smiled to herself and ignored it. She missed her parents and was looking forward to the next time she could get away to Florida to visit them.

"I'm getting promoted," Raegan whispered excitedly into the phone.

"Whisper louder, Momma can't hear you baby," Her mother said, nearly screaming into the phone.

"I'm getting a promotion," Raegan said, whispering as loud as she could without using her speaking voice. The walls were thin and Michelle's office was right next to hers and she always seemed to be listening to what was going on in Raegan's office.

"You're getting a devotion? What do you mean you're getting a devotion? Oh, wait, did you say promotion?" her mom screamed into the phone. "Frank, our baby is getting a promotion!"

"That's right, Mom! There are a couple of contingencies but I'm feeling pretty good about it."

"That is so good baby! Momma is so proud of you. When are you coming home again? We'll have to celebrate you when you get here and maybe you can talk some sense into Eric. He is still playing around out there at that old college. I swear that child is going to make a career out of going to college."

"Mom, he is going to get it together. He just decided on a major. He says he is passionate about children learning so he is going to study education so that he can teach," Raegan said, defending her younger brother.

"Yeah, he's told your father and me that but we just hope he sticks with it this time. These funds are going to dry up because we aren't going to pay for him to go to college forever. We're retired now so we don't have a boatload of money to throw at him while he plays around in school chasing skirts," Raegan's mother ranted.

Laughing, because she could see her mom's facial expression clearly as she ranted on about her brother, Raegan said, "He is going to be fine, Mom. It just took him a while to find his way. I have faith in him."

"We're just worried about him. We would like to see him graduate before we leave this earth."

"He'll be graduating in a couple of years; you guys just need to hold on. Hold on for much longer after he graduates now."

"All right baby, I'm about to make lunch for your daddy. I will call you when I think you're home from work or you can call me on your way home like you usually do."

"Okay, Mommy, I love you. Give Daddy a hug and kiss for me."

"All right baby. Enjoy the rest of your workday."

"Thanks Mommy."

Glad to have shared the news with her mom, all she could now think about was sharing it with Caleb. She wondered how he would celebrate her.

CHAPTER 23

∞

"Hello, this is Raegan." Raegan picked up her desk phone. She was so caught up in her work that she didn't glance at the number displayed in the caller ID window.

"Hello, gorgeous." Rico was on the line. She couldn't help but feel slightly disappointed. Part of her wanted it to be Caleb, but that was silly because he didn't have her work number.

"Oh, hi! How have you been? How was the rest of the convention?" Raegan hadn't spoken with Rico in a few days. In fact, she was avoiding him, using work as an excuse. She needed time to sort out her feelings and she couldn't do that by spending time with him.

"It was good; just the usual business of the fraternity. I haven't really spoken with you much since you came to meet me and the guys at the restaurant. I needed to hear your beautiful voice and check on you. Are you good?" His deep voice echoed through the line.

"Yes, I am. I'm sorry I haven't been as available. Things have been very busy at work and are going to get a little busier."

"Sounds like you're getting more responsibility? That could be a good thing. Is it?"

"I think it is! I'm hoping for a promotion soon, so I have to make sure I own these extra assignments," She said without giving any details of the recent news she received regarding her upcoming promotion. She wasn't feeling very connected with him, so she wasn't compelled to share it.

"As I know you will. You're so amazing. Now everybody knows it," he said, flattering her.

Smiling from ear to ear, she thanked him, exchanged a few more pleasantries and ended the call. She didn't want to risk the chance of the conversation moving towards Caleb. She knew that Rico hadn't quite let the situation go and she didn't want to talk about it over the phone. Or ever.

Just as she ended the call, Michelle knocked on the door as she entered and shut the door behind her.

"Kensi told me that you saw Caleb at Buffalo Wild Wings with Rico. Oooh, what was that about?" Michelle sang. She was anxious to hear the juicy details. "You've been holding out on me. I've been trying to see how long it would take you to spill the beans, but obviously you weren't going to say a thing, were you?" Michelle said, leaning against the door with folded arms, squinting her eyes at Raegan.

"Of course I was planning to tell you about it!" Raegan said, partially relieved. When Michelle first entered the door, she assumed that she wanted to hear about Raegan's performance review. She should have known better.

"Really, Rae? It's already Wednesday afternoon. How many days has it been?" Before Raegan could answer, Michelle continued. "Too many. Now tell me what's going on. How did you feel?" Michelle asked as she got comfortable in Raegan's office, sitting in the only guest chair, crossing her legs and sliding the chair closer to Raegan's desk as if she was about to hear a titillating story.

"Of course, I was pretty upset and confused when I first saw him. It didn't even click that he would be here at the fraternity convention. Even so, what were the odds of me seeing him? This city is huge!" Raegan said, exaggerating with her arms stretched wide.

"Umm hmm. And?" Michelle said as she waved her hand to usher her on.

"Now don't sit here acting like you don't know the story. You know I know that Kensi told you. She did not just say, 'oh, Raegan saw Caleb' and provide no further details," Raegan said, sitting back in her leather seat with folded arms.

"Of course not, but it isn't the same as hearing the story directly from you," Michelle said, pointing at her.

Raegan shared the weekend events with Michelle, recounting as much about her time spent with Caleb as she remembered, from the moment she saw him at the restaurant with Rico to their time together at Char. The detail Michelle wanted to know most was what really happened when they broke up, and so Raegan told her Caleb's side of the story.

Raegan was interested in hearing what someone else thought since she has been known to be a little unreasonable. She wanted to make sure that she didn't make any silly decisions again when it came to Caleb.

"I'm glad that you two got a chance to talk things through. It's been way too long. I'm surprised that you allowed it to go on this long." Michelle had to rethink that. She wasn't really surprised since Raegan was known for holding grudges. "Didn't Kendrick have a thing for you anyway?" Michelle asked, reminding Raegan that she probably should have questioned Kendrick when he mentioned that Caleb was cheating on her. Especially since Kendrick was intoxicated; she should have never taken his word for it.

"I'm going to get it together. As far as Kendrick having a thing for me, I don't know. Caleb seems to think so. How do you know that anyway?" Pausing for a second, she said, "Oh, yeah…Kensi."

"So the bigger question is, where does this leave you two? Where does it leave Rico? Have you thought about that?" Michelle asked the questions that had been plaguing Raegan.

"Well, actually, nothing has changed except that we've decided to work on being friends. Rico is still my beau. Nothing else has changed." If Raegan was being honest, the truth is that *everything* had changed. The man that she once thought she would spend the rest of her life with, before Damian, had come back into her life.

"If you say so. Everyone knows that you were head over heels in love with Caleb. Now that things are kosher again, you think you can just continue on with life as if nothing has changed?" Michelle asked skeptically. She and Raegan sat in silence for a moment.

"That's the plan. I can't just stop seeing Rico because of Caleb's story. It's been so long, I don't think it's worth holding on to, even if the story is true. I can't lie and say that I'm not happy about hearing that he wasn't cheating and I honestly feel a little silly about never hearing what he had to say. But that was ten years ago; it's time to move on," she said, talking more to herself than to Michelle. She didn't know who she was trying to convince more.

"All right, I'm going to remember this conversation. I just hope you remember it too," Michelle said, wagging her finger at Raegan.

"No need," Raegan said holding her hand in the air. "Have you forgotten that Rico may be the one?"

"Have you forgotten that Caleb was the one?" Michelle challenged her.

"Don't you have work to do?" Raegan said in an attempt to get Michelle out of her office.

"Nope. Don't try to kick me out of your office because you don't want to hear the truth. You know that in the near future, you will have to make some choices about this whole relationship thing. I won't push you though. Let's just see how this all plays out. In fact, I'm interested in seeing what happens, probably more than you are. I need popcorn for this movie," Michelle said teasingly.

"I'm so sure of it." Raegan leaned back in her chair, arms folded.

"But hey, I know when I'm not wanted," Michelle said, standing and walking towards the door. "I'm going to pack up and get out of here early. I will work late tomorrow to make up for today."

"Thanks for the chat but I actually do have a few things that I need to get done before I leave for the day. I will give you a call later."

"See you."

Michelle was starting to sound a lot like Raegan's conscience. She knew that she would have decisions to make and the decisions would probably be a lot easier if she had not broken her celibacy and given herself to Rico. She had been such a fool but she was hoping that her silliness would somehow pay off and that maybe he was the one for her. But now Caleb was back and she wasn't so sure if she *wanted* Rico to be the one anymore. She was confident God would lead her so she'd let it go for now.

CHAPTER 24

∞

After getting ready for the basketball game and having a pep talk with Raegan, Tammy left her hotel room to wait in the lobby for the car to pick her up. *Time passes so quickly, especially when you're nervous,* she thought. The car would be there any minute.

As soon as she arrived downstairs and walked towards the front of the hotel, through the glass doors she saw the car pulling up.

"It's showtime," she said, taking a deep breath to calm her nerves.

She rode in the backseat of the car in silence, trying to rehearse what she would say to Josh when she finally saw him. As she was muddling through her thoughts, the car pulled up in front of the basketball stadium.

"Ma'am, we've arrived at your destination," the driver said, glancing at her through the rearview mirror.

"Whoa, that was quick," she said, reaching in her purse to hand him a tip. He walked around to her door to open it for her. He reached for her hand to help her out of the car and she handed the bill to him, but he refused.

"Oh, no ma'am, everything has already been taken care of by Mr. Gary's company."

"But I insist," she said, placing the bill in his jacket and walked away.

"Thanks ma'am. Please have Mr. Gary give me a call when you're ready to leave."

"Will do," she said as she walked up to the stadium. She noticed Gary standing off to the side, waiting for her. He was dressed in a green polo shirt, in an effort to show his support for the home team, and black slacks. It looked as if he'd just had a haircut. When she approached him, she got a whiff of his Armani cologne. *He smelled great*, she thought.

"Hello," Tammy said, reaching into her purse. "Here are the tickets. Are you ready for some fun?"

"Certainly," he said, holding out his arm to escort her to their seats.

They arrived about one hour before the game started, so they had time to grab a snack, settle into their seats and watch the players warm up. She ordered a hotdog, nachos, beer and water. She didn't drink beer but decided to order one to make the client feel comfortable. She didn't drink it; she just nursed the bottle throughout the game while sipping on her water. As they were sitting in their seats, discussing everything from work to basketball to family, she could feel someone's eyes on her. Before even meeting those eyes with her own, she already knew who they belonged to. Her skin grew warm as she glanced up to meet Josh's gaze.

Josh couldn't believe that Tammy was there to watch his game. She had only been to one of his games before their separation, so he had to make sure that he was on top of his game tonight.

She waved at him and mouthed, "Hey."

The client didn't miss the exchange and asked, "Do you know Joshua Archer?"

"Yes, I know him," she said without explanation and took another sip of water. She didn't think it was necessary to mention that they were legally separated.

"That's amazing! You have to introduce me to him after the game!" Gary said. He could tell by her tone and lack of eye contact that she didn't want to discuss how she knew Josh so he left it alone. However, he didn't plan to let that stop him from meeting him. Gary commented, "There is no way we can leave this stadium without me getting a personal introduction and an autograph!" He was even more excited about the game now.

She started making some weird hand symbols while trying to mouth, "Come see us after the game." Joshua didn't understand anything she was trying to do. She was starting to look like she was losing her mind. He had no idea what kind of gang signs she was throwing up. Luckily for her, the buzzer sounded as it was time for them to return to the locker room to get ready for game time. Oh his way to the locker room, he stopped by their seats to say hello. He was briefly caught off guard by seeing her with another man, because technically, she was still his wife. However, before he could finish the suspicious thought, she told him that she was there for business and she was entertaining a client, Gary. She asked him to meet them after the game because Gary was a huge fan and wanted to meet him and get his autograph. He agreed and shuffled into the locker room to meet the rest of the team.

"This is so awesome! Tammy, we're going to have to be business partners forever after this," Gary said with a light chuckle.

Great! she thought. This would certainly go over well with the partners. It was starting to work out for her after all.

Moments later, the announcer came over the loud speaker to ask the crowd to stand as someone came out to sing the national anthem. As soon as that was over, the announcer began calling out the names of the starting players for each team. She had to admit that she felt a tinge of excitement as he called out Joshua's name. She was happy that he was able to follow his dreams but a little down that they couldn't work out anything to where she could share in it with him. She just felt like there wasn't enough room in his life for basketball and her.

"So, Tammy, how often do you get a chance to attend Celtics games since you know Josh Archer?"

"Actually, not often. I haven't been to one of these games in years. Work and other commitments usually keep me busy," she lied. There was no need for Gary to know that she was still technically married to the guy. In fact, that was one little thing about herself that she preferred for others not to know. She felt like that was one of her biggest failures and she surely didn't want to highlight it.

Throughout the game, they cheered and chatted about everything. Gary was actually a pretty swell guy and she was glad that her company had him as a client. It was good to work with an honest, hard-working person. She couldn't say the same thing about a lot of their clients. Many of them were greedy businessmen who only cared about the money and not about the value of their people.

At half-time, Tammy excused herself to go to the restroom and send a quick text to Raegan, just to give her an update.

"Things are going well. He spotted us before the game started. He came over to speak. Will see him after the game to introduce him to client," she texted.

Immediately, Raegan responded, "Good deal. Keep me posted. I can't wait to hear the juice! Have fun!"

That was fast; I guess she really was hugging that phone. She smiled and thought to herself. She was happy that she could have someone to confide in and support her. Raegan was such a great friend. After using the restroom and heading back to her seat, she noticed that she had a few more minutes and went to grab more snacks and another beer for Gary.

Heading back to her seat, she was greeted by Gary's bright smile and wide eyes. He was enjoying the game as well as her company. *She was such a beautiful woman with a great attitude*, he thought.

"Hey, I figured I would bring more snacks and another beer for you," She said, handing over the items.

"Great! Thank you. I was just about to stop the guy over there to grab another beer. That was thoughtful and much appreciated."

"You're welcome." She was amazed at how much alcohol many of her clients could drink. They had such a high tolerance; it was almost shameful. She was happy that Gary seemed to have control and was not over doing it. He was on his third beer and she was hoping it would be the last. She didn't want things to become inappropriate, especially since he was a valued client.

"You're just in time; half-time is almost over," Gary said, popping the top off the bottle of beer. He took a swig and smiled at her.

"Oh good. This is such a great game tonight. Don't you think so?" Tammy asked. She was doing her best to focus on the client and not worry about how things would transpire between her and Joshua later.

"Of course! And it doesn't hurt one bit that our team is winning! These are such great seats. Thank your management team for me," he said with a slight wink.

"No, thank you for agreeing to come along. It's our pleasure to see to it that our clients are taken care of," she said. Not only was Gary being taken care of tonight; she hoped to take care of a little business of her own.

They cheered and chatted through the second half of the game. Her heart raced each time Joshua had the ball, dribbling up and down the court or taking a shot. She was excited and nervous for him. He was great at basketball and was one of the best shooters for his team. When the game ended, she and Gary remained seated and continued to talk until the players went to freshen up and return to the arena. A rush of anxiety came over her when she noticed Josh approaching their seats. He stopped right in front of her and stretched his arms wide so that he could embrace her. She slowly stood and walked into his embrace. That was one of the best hugs she had in a long time, although sweaty. It felt good to have Josh close again. After what seemed like an eternity, she backed away and found Gary standing and waiting to be introduced. Gary went on about how he was a big fan of the Celtics and Josh. He had followed his career since he started in the NBA right out of college. The guys talked about basketball for a bit until Tammy interrupted them.

"Josh, it was great seeing you. Gary, we'll be in touch. I am going to head on back to my hotel room now," she said, grabbing her purse from the seat. She wondered if Josh would try to stop her.

"Tammy, you're invited to party with us. We always celebrate after winning a game," Josh said, never taking his eyes off of her. Gary watched the exchange.

"Thanks, but I'm pretty tired. I have a car waiting for me outside, I think. Gary, did you call your driver?" she asked, turning to him. She hoped Joshua would take the hint that she didn't want Gary involved in her business.

"I sure did," Gary said, reassuring her that the arrangements were taken care of. "He should be here now." Gary glanced at his watch noting how much time had passed since he placed the call.

"Can I please have one last hug?" Joshua asked, sensing that she wanted to remain professional. Tammy obliged and embraced him again before leaving. Gary shook Josh's hand once more and asked for his autograph. Both pleased that the night turned out well, Tammy and Gary joined what was left of the crowd and exited the arena. Gary walked her to the car, though she would have preferred Josh; she wanted to play it cool because she didn't want the client in her business like that.

CHAPTER 25

∞

Thoughts of how she would handle things with Caleb and Rico consumed Raegan's thoughts. She wished that the answer would just fall into her lap but she knew that she had to live through this, use wisdom and make these tough choices to the best of her ability.

To give herself time to think, she decided to relax in a tub of water as warm as she could stand it, filled with bubbles. Just as she was running her bubble bath, her phone rang again. It was Caleb. A smile instantly spread across her face. She should not have been so excited for another guy to be calling her, but she was. It was late, so she spent a few seconds debating whether or not she should answer the phone. What could he want at this hour anyway? She was curious and she really wanted to hear his voice, so she answered, telling herself she would only talk for a few minutes. That couldn't hurt anything.

"Hello," Raegan said. She held her breath waiting for him to speak.

"Raegan Camille, how are you?" Caleb's voice caressed her ears through the phone.

"I'm great," she said, smiling as she slowly released the pent up breath. Raegan tried hard not to let her smile become evident in her voice.

"What are you up to?" Caleb asked. He was relieved that she answered his call. He knew it was a little late and didn't want to give her the wrong impression. However, he thought it was worth the risk just to hear her voice before going to bed. A voice that he missed for the last ten years.

"About to take a bath, getting ready for bed. I do have to work in the morning, you know?" Raegan said, testing the warm water with her foot.

"Do you need to go then?" he asked, hoping she would stay on the phone.

"No, not yet. What's up?" she asked as she slipped into the warm water. She masked her pleasure at the silky feel of the water against her skin. She didn't want Caleb to get any ideas.

"I had a late night at the office. I'm heading home now. You were on my mind so I thought I would give you a call." He had missed her every moment since he returned to Georgia.

"I appreciate that," she said as she rested her head on the tub pillow and relaxed in the warm bubbly water. "So why were you thinking about me? What's on your mind?"

"Because...I hope to get to see you when I come your way again in a couple of weeks," He said. He listened closely for her response.

"Oh, why will you be out here?" she asked. Her heart began to race at the possibilities. He obviously didn't realize that she was still in a relationship with Rico . . . or maybe it was her that didn't realize it.

"I'll be looking for a place," he said, dropping the news on her bit by bit.

Raegan quickly sat up in the tub. "What do you mean?" she asked, becoming confused.

"Remember when I discussed wanting new opportunities over dessert?"

"Yeah..."

"Well, I have one. The company is starting a new unit out there and they want me to lead it. So it looks like we'll be in the same city." There. He said it.

Her eyes widened as her mouth dropped open. She didn't know what to say. All she could think about was that she was going to somehow have to tell Rico something about this whole situation because it was not going away now. What did all of this mean? She was getting ahead of herself so she decided to let it go and live in the moment of the conversation that she was having with him. The word "congratulations" slipped out of her mouth. She wasn't sure if she meant it or not.

"Thanks! I'm pretty excited about it. I hope this means that I will somehow get a chance to see more of you," Caleb said hopefully.

"I am still dating Rico," Raegan said to convince both Caleb and herself.

"Oh, yeah. That's right. I'll be around when that's over," he said laughing.

"Whatever. What kind of friend are you? Encouraging my relationship to end."

"I'm probably the best friend you have. I know that there is something, well someone, out there much better for you, but you need to see that for yourself. I will be waiting when you do," said Caleb.

"Yeah, right. Sure. If you're not a better friend you won't be around," she said, scooping bubbles and blowing them off her hand.

"What are you doing for Thanksgiving?" Caleb asked, changing the subject.

"I'm going to Florida to visit my family. What about you?"

"I'm going to Florida to visit my family, too. It's been a while since I've been home to see them. I've been working quite a bit lately, especially with taking on this new project."

"I can certainly understand that. I have something similar going on myself."

"Wow. Really?" he asked, genuinely excited for her. He knew how much she enjoyed her work and wanted the best for her both professionally and in her personal life.

"Yes! It's not quite official yet but I'm getting promoted to manager!"

"You and I both know that you're great at what you do, and if they mentioned anything to you, it is as official as the grass is green," he said, showering her with compliments about her work. He knew that she worked hard and was committed to moving up in her career.

"Ha. I guess so. The promotion is mine as soon as my performance review is official."

"That's awesome! I'm going to take you out to celebrate when I return."

"I don't know how much Rico will like that."

"Who says that he has to like it?" he countered.

"There you go not being a good friend again," she said, sounding as if she was singing the words.

"Actually, I'm being an excellent friend—inviting you out to celebrate your accomplishments. Right? Isn't that what friends do?"

"You know exactly what I mean, Caleb."

"Yes, I do but that doesn't mean that I will stop trying," he said before exchanging "good night" wishes and ending the call. He pulled into his driveway, passing the "For Sale" sign in his yard. He was going to miss his home but he was excited about this new opportunity. He now had a chance for his career and love life to really take off, and he wasn't going down without a fight.

CHAPTER 26

∞

Whew. After speaking with Caleb, Raegan spent a few more minutes soaking in the tub while allowing her thoughts to take over. *Why is this relationship thing becoming so complicated?* She knew that it was her making it complicated. It really didn't have to be. She was with Rico and that was all there was to it—except that it wasn't. Caleb somehow found himself back in the picture and now she just might have to choose.

She didn't want to lose Caleb again. Although they weren't together, he had made his intentions clear. She had history with Caleb. He knew her and she knew him. She thought it easy to build from the past that they once shared. The more she thought about Caleb, the more her doubts rose about Rico.

Caleb made her question her relationship with Rico, not because of Caleb's thoughts about Rico but because of her feelings for Caleb. She wondered if she would still feel the same if she didn't have any feelings for Caleb. Would her doubts about Rico still exist? What if the doubts she had about Rico were somehow erased—would she still love Caleb? Did she only love Caleb because of her doubts about Rico, and Caleb was potentially a safe place for her? Was she simply holding on to what she had with Caleb before the incident and hoping things could be as they once were? So many questions. Very few answers.

Her thoughts were quickly interrupted by the phone ringing again. She peered over the tub to see who the caller was: It was Rico. She wasn't as excited as she used to be. What had happened? She pressed the "on" button on her Bluetooth and answered the phone.

"Hey cupcake, what's up?" Raegan said as she answered the phone, feigning as much excitement as she could.

"Cupcake?" he asked laughing. "That's new. That sounds fruity, so I don't know if I like that."

"Shouldn't you just be happy that I have a pet name for you?" she asked.

"No. You need to find something fitting."

"I think you should be grateful that I think you're as sweet as cupcakes."

"Nice try. What are you doing?"

"Finishing up a bubble bath so that I can hit the sheets."

"I wish that I could join you."

"What are you doing?" she asked, purposely ignoring his comment. She had gone down that road several times before with Rico and it was definitely time that she got herself together. She needed to recommit herself to celibacy and keep her mind and heart clear. She had way too much going on in the relationship department. She needed to be sure that her judgment wasn't clouded by sex.

"Just finished watching the game. I wanted to call and wish you sweet dreams before going to bed myself. I have a long day tomorrow."

"Thanks sweetness," She said. She didn't engage him when he spoke of his upcoming long day. She just wasn't interested. Her mind was still swirling with thoughts of Caleb.

"Are we still on for dinner and a movie this weekend? I feel like it's been forever since we've spent quality time together," Rico said.

Rico was right. Raegan had been busy with her new responsibilities at work and hadn't made any time for him. It's not that she couldn't have, it's just that she didn't. She believed that everyone made time for what they wanted; but she wasn't sure what she wanted so she buried herself in her work.

"Yes. What time are you picking me up?"

"I will be at your house at 6:30, so please be ready lady," Rico said. He always had to wait for her so he felt the need to make his request known since he was making reservations.

"I will do my best. Good night."

"Good night. I love you."

"I love you too," Raegan whispered into the phone as she ended the call. She didn't know if she believed that anymore. *Oh, this is definitely not good,* she thought. She decided not to give the situation too much more thought and to get some rest. She had to participate in recruiting events at three different colleges this week, and she needed to be at her very best.

The week passed quickly and the next thing Raegan knew, it was time for her to prepare for her date with Rico. She figured that since they hadn't had a chance to talk, tonight would be a good time to bring up some of the issues plaguing her about him. With all of this talk about marriage and her being the one, it was time to put him to the test and discuss some serious issues—one of them being money.

CHAPTER 27

∞

As soon as Tammy arrived back at her hotel, Joshua called. She should have known that he wouldn't waste any time.

"Hey, pack your things. I'm sending a car for you," Joshua said to her.

"I am not in the mood to go out partying with you and your basketball friends and groupies," Tammy said as she plopped down on the bed and kicked off her shoes.

"Did I say that we were going out? You're coming to my house. You are still my wife; you can't stay in a hotel." He meant every word of that. He thought they should be together and he wanted to start working on them being an *us* again. He promised that to himself and her grandmother.

"Not if you're sending a car for me. If you want me, come by and pick me up yourself. I'm staying at the Ritz near the arena," Tammy said. She knew she was being stubborn but just wanted him to prove that she was important enough for him to do the job himself.

"I have no problem with that. I just passed by. I will circle the block and come back to the valet entrance to meet you," Joshua said, meeting her challenge. He knew Tammy was trying to test him and he didn't have a problem with that. He figured it was about time they start trying to patch things up.

"Okay." She was actually quite surprised. She didn't think that he would go for that but he did. She was sure that he had gotten used to throwing his money around, but she knew the real Joshua and she wasn't going to have it. He was going to have to work way more than his money in order to get her back. (And that was exactly what she wanted—she wanted him to try to win her heart back.)

She packed essentials for the night and work the next morning and headed right back out of her hotel room. She didn't check out because it was customary to stay in the hotel room while on a business trip. If she checked out, there would have been questions as to where she stayed for the rest of the time here, and she preferred to keep this part of her life private for the time being.

Her heart was pacing as she walked back towards the elevators. It had been nearly nine years since she had even been in the same room with him, let alone such confined quarters as a car. As the elevator dinged passing each floor, her heart matched it with loud pounding.

"Get it together girl. He is still Josh," she said to her reflection in the mirrored elevator panels. As she gave herself a pep talk, she checked her hair and makeup right before exiting and walking to the valet area. He was already there. *Here goes nothing*, she thought.

To her surprise, he got out of the car to come around and open the door for her. She was sure he would be trying to avoid the spotlight and cameras with the cellphone-picture-taking frenzy going on these days, but he wasn't. He didn't care; his Tammy was there.

"Thanks," she said, smiling from ear to ear, showcasing her freshly cleaned teeth and earth-tone lip color.

"Anything for you," he said closing her car door. In just a few strides, he was getting back into the car to drive home.

He immediately began speaking. "Tammy, I was so surprised to see you sitting on the sideline tonight. It's been a long time. But why didn't you tell me you were coming?"

"I don't know. I suppose I wanted to surprise you. I honestly didn't think I would have time to see you and then this came up. I had to entertain the client, so I figured it would be an excellent opportunity to show him a good time and get a chance to see one of your games live."

"We just spoke a few weeks ago; you should have told me you were coming. I could have made plans for us. How long are you here?"

"I'm leaving first thing Friday morning."

"And how long have you been here?" he asked, taking a quick glance at her as he continued to navigate the highway.

"Since Sunday afternoon," she said sheepishly.

"That's cold, Tammy." He couldn't believe that she had been in town all of this time and didn't even call to say hello. He didn't really expect that of her since she had been pretty selfish in their relationship in the past, but he still thought that was the polite thing to do. He would have done if it he were in Houston. In fact, he calls her every time he plays in Houston, Dallas or San Antonio.

"Clearly, you were getting ready for your game; you wouldn't have had time to meet with me," Tammy said, defending her actions. Once again, Tammy was making decisions for Joshua, thinking that she knew how he felt. She honestly believed things were easier this way.

He immediately remembered what tore them apart years ago and decided not to get into it, because that was exactly where the conversation was headed. He adored Tammy and could have made time for her but she didn't feel that way. He hoped they were both more mature now and could handle being with each other while furthering both of their careers. He didn't see any reason why they couldn't do that. He figured that he would only play a few more years and then retire to become a sports analyst or something.

"Well, I'm glad I'm getting a chance to see you now. You look gorgeous!" he said as he removed his right hand from the steering wheel and placed it on top of her thigh.

"Thank you," she said, trying to hide the blushing of her cheeks. But she did nothing to remove his hand from her thigh.

"Is there anything you would like to do or see before you go? I have plans of my own for you if you can't think of anything. And before you even think it, I'm not talking about sex. ..I called and had my maid prepare something just for us. It should be ready by the time we get there," he said with a teasing smile.

"I'm all for that then; I'd like to see what you have planned," she said, taking a moment to think about what he'd just said. "How could you be so sure that I would come with you?"

"I wasn't sure, just hopeful. I would have just enjoyed it by myself if you didn't come," he said as he shrugged his shoulders.

She wasn't sure how true that was, especially since she *knew* most athletes found someone to keep them company. She was certain he could find someone to spend the time with.

The drive lasted about forty-five minutes. As they rode to his house, they discussed both of their careers, family, college and old times. It seemed as if he was maturing into a great man, she mused.

When they arrived at his home, all she could muster up was, "Wow." His home was huge and the landscaping was beautiful. His yard was adorned with beautiful lights surrounding a Toscana fountain.

"This is gorgeous," she said.

"The backyard is even nicer. Let me show you." He grabbed her hand and led her to the backyard to show her the beautiful landscaping. It looked like something from an HGTV magazine, rich and famous edition. It was huge. The grass was freshly manicured, covered stone patio with an outside kitchen, fireplace, gazebo and hot tub.

"Who is your landscaper?" she asked as if she was going to need his services.

"I hired some guy that, apparently, everyone in the neighborhood uses. I got his information from my neighbor."

"Well, he did a fantastic job!"

"Thanks. I sit out here from time to time just to relax and think. I know you must think I live some kind of wild life but it's actually relatively calm outside of basketball games," Joshua spoke to the thoughts swirling around in her head.

She simply smiled as she looked up into his eyes. She wasn't asking for an explanation but she was certain that he was only telling her what he thought she wanted to hear. After admiring the beauty in his backyard, she walked back to the door and placed her hand in his so that he could lead her into his home.

His home was nice but she didn't notice much of the décor because the lights were dimmed and candles lined the entryway to the kitchen. On the table was a setting for two with plates covered by silver tops. Flowers, candles, a bottle of wine and two wine glasses were already placed on the table.

"What is this?" she asked inhaling the sweet aroma that flowed from the table.

"Your favorite things, from what I remember."

He took her coat and purse and put them aside, pulled out her chair so that she could sit, and uncovered her plate. It was her favorites: grilled shrimp, tilapia topped with crab and wine butter sauce, steamed broccoli and her favorite bottle of wine. It was very appealing to the eye. *Room service has nothing on this,* she thought.

"This looks amazing! How did you get this set up so fast? Nevermind, don't answer that."

He took his seat, prayed and they began eating and chatting. As they sat and talked, they were reminded of the happier times in their marriage. Everything was so natural for the two of them, and they both had to admit that they missed that. After dinner, they headed upstairs to the master suite that was equally as gorgeous as the landscaping. The bathroom itself was as large as her living room and kitchen combined. It was such a great space. There were his and her closets in the bathroom that were about the size of her bedroom. His and her sinks. Separate tub and shower. Jetted tub. The shower was so large that there were three shower heads and a sitting area. The entire bathroom was covered in marble.

"I was just going to take a quick shower but I must relax in this tub! You don't mind, do you?" she asked. There was no way she could pass up reveling in such beauty.

"Of course not, as long as I can sit in here with you and continue our talk. Not in the tub but just sitting next to you. I have bubbles if you still like those," he said as he took a few long strides over to the cabinet to grab the bottle of luxury bath beads and liquid.

"Certainly." She noticed that they were her favorite lavender scented bubbles, unopened. "Let me guess. Did you have those picked up moments ago as well?"

"I did. I knew you would love this setup and would like to relax in here," Joshua said, gesturing toward the open space.

"All for this one moment! Yes! Thank you," she said as she began to set her water just the way she liked it. Josh stepped away while Tammy prepared the bubble bath.

After Tammy climbed the steps into the tub and sat down to relax in the hot, bubbly water, she called out to him to return. He pulled a bench closer to the tub and took a seat to finish their conversation. They continued their talk, going into depth about everything that had been going on with them for the last few years. Although they talked on the phone from time to time, they never really exchanged much more than mere pleasantries. It felt good to unwind and talk with Josh. *He was an excellent communicator these days. Where was this guy years ago*, she thought.

After her nice, long soak, he exited the bathroom so that she could towel dry and get dressed. As much as he wanted to stay, he didn't want Tammy to think he was trying to pressure her into sex, especially after the great time they were having. Once dressed, she met him in the master bedroom where she stretched across that extra soft bed and made herself really comfortable. *These must be 10,000 count sheets,* she thought, if there were such a thing. He lay close to her and they continued to talk late into the night until falling asleep.

CHAPTER 28

∞

Joshua was already awake preparing breakfast when Tammy woke up. *Has he always been this thoughtful?* she wondered. *Have I been missing out on something great?* They continued to catch up through breakfast as they took advantage of their last moments. She needed to get to work before 9:00 a.m., and luckily for her, she still had about one and a half hours. He was all set to take her to work but she stopped him.

"Where are you going? You know I can't let you drive me to work. People are going to talk," she said as she held up her hand, stopping him in his tracks.

"I don't care about that. You're only here for a short time and other people are the last thing on my mind." He continued to insist and she eventually relented and allowed him to drive.

"If it will make you feel any better, I will drive the Buick Enclave. The windows are tinted and no one will ever know. Does that work for you?" He held the keys in the air.

"I guess… I can't believe you're driving an Enclave though. I figured you'd want something more expensive." Other than the large, beautiful home, Tammy was a little surprised that he wasn't living a lavish lifestyle.

"It's expensive enough. Just because I have a lot of money doesn't mean I have to spend it all, especially on a vehicle. I have to plan for my future and that of my wife, children and grandchildren. I'm thinking generational. This isn't just about me, you know." Joshua explained.

"You're right. I suppose most athletes can learn something from you," She commended him.

"The garage is this way; let's get you to the office on time." And he did just that. They made it to the office about fifteen minutes before 9:00. Traffic wasn't as bad as they both thought it would be. As he pulled around to the front of the building, he prepared to get out of the car to open her door but he was met with resistance from her again.

"No, don't do that. Remember, I don't want to bring any extra attention to either of us. Thank you for everything," she said, grabbing her things to get out of the car.

Grabbing her hand before she reached to let herself out, he asked, "Can I see you later? I know you're leaving tomorrow, but I really would like to see you again before you go."

"Sure. I should have a pretty short workday today as I'm wrapping things up out here. I will call you when I make it back to my hotel room."

"Thanks. I'm going to stick around town. I will probably go practice on my game and wait for you to call me," Joshua said leaning forward for a kiss.

"I look forward to it," she said as she placed a quick kiss on his lips and hopped out of the car. Tammy felt so relaxed and optimistic; she was bound to have a great day.

She only worked half a day and went back to her hotel room to call Josh. Before she could make a call, her phone started ringing. She was giddy thinking that Joshua was calling to check on her.

Looking at the caller ID, she became concerned. It was her mom. Her mom never called in the middle of the day. With shaky hands, she answered the phone. Her concern grew as she heard the reason for the call—her grandmother was sick again and the doctors thought it would probably be a good idea to call the family in. Tammy moved mechanically to sit on the edge of the bed as she listened to the details her mother was giving her. Immediately her world shifted.

Her grandmother practically raised her as she stayed with her during the summers when her mom and dad were working. She had just spoken to her about a week ago and she seemed fine. But now the lung cancer had taken a turn for the worse and Tammy had to make sure she got home in time. She immediately packed her things, checked out of the hotel and hailed a taxicab to the airport. She didn't even think to call Josh because she was so preoccupied with the reality that she might never see her grandmother alive again. While in the taxi, she called the airline to see when the next available flight would be. The flight was in two hours and there were five seats left. They changed her ticket for her while she was en route. That was just enough time for her to get to the airport, check her bags, go through security and wait to board the flight.

She wasn't prepared for this at all. She couldn't compose herself and she allowed the tears to flow as she sat in the airport terminal waiting to board her flight.

Tammy sent a text to Raegan letting her know that she would be arriving early and asked if she would be able to pick her up. After confirming everything with Raegan, she tried to relax as much as possible. She had a two-and-a-half-hour flight back home and she prayed to God that He would allow her to get there in enough time to see Granny once more, since her health was failing fast. As soon as she finished praying, she received another phone call, but from her cousin this time, updating her on their granny's condition.

"How does she look?" Tammy asked. She remained still, holding her breath, in an effort to brace herself for her cousin's response.

"She doesn't look good, Tammy. But she's still alert and talking, and doesn't seem to be in much pain. And she's asking for you. Are you coming home today?"

"Yes, I'm actually on the next flight out of here."

"Okay, please be careful. Granny knows you're coming; she is going to hang on for you. You know that."

Why do people say things like that? she thought. *How do they know?* It was so nerve wracking and frustrating. She was starting to get a headache from worry. Just then, a flight attendant came over the speaker asking passengers to prepare to board. She was happy that she was able to keep her first-class seating; she didn't feel like waiting to board the plane today.

The flight was pretty smooth and without incident. She arrived at baggage claim to find that Raegan was waiting for her with open arms. Raegan squeezed her tight as if to let her know that it was okay to cry.

"Listen to me Tammy; it's going to be all right. You have me to lean on if you need to do so. Let's get you to the hospital," Raegan said as she and her friend walked arm in arm out of the baggage claim area and to her car.

At the hospital, Raegan walked with Tammy to her grandmother's room. Tammy's feet were feeling heavier and her heart was thumping so loudly that she could feel the pulsation in her ears. She was so afraid to lose her grandmother but she was also very sad for her mom. Her mom was her grandmother's youngest child and also the closest one to her. She had spent the last few months taking care of her during her illness. This was going to be so hard for both of them.

When they arrived at her grandmother's room, Raegan told her that she would be outside in the hallway if Tammy needed her. Raegan released her friend's arm and watched as she slowly entered the cold room. Raegan took a seat outside in the hallway and waited.

"Hey Granny, I'm here," Tammy said, trying her best to smile through her pain. She walked timidly into the room as if the sound of her footsteps would set off some sort of alarm.

"How are you baby? Come on over here and let me look at you," her grandmother said. She edged closer to the bed and her grandmother's slender fingers grabbed hers as if she knew she would never hold her hands again. "You look so good. I still can't understand how you walk around in those high heel shoes all the time. I never could do that," she said in between long ragged breaths.

Tammy couldn't hold back the tears. She quickly wiped away the tears that escaped from her eyes and placed her hands back into her granny's hands. She wanted to be strong for her grandmother but everyone knew what would soon happen. It would be the end for them but the beginning of peace for Granny.

Her grandmother placed her hands on Tammy's cheek and asked her not to cry, encouraging her by telling her that everything would be all right.

"I'm going to see my Lord, baby," Her grandmother said, smiling weakly. She recalled hearing her grandmother sing that line many times while growing up.

The cancer had really gotten the best of her as she could tell by looking at the thin hospital gown clinging to her grandmother's body. Tammy was heartbroken. How could it have come to this? Not her Granny.

The doctor came into the room to examine Tammy's grandmother. Tammy stepped out of the room for a moment because it was too much for her to stomach. She slumped down beside Raegan in the empty chair and breathed a long sigh.

"What do you do when death is so close that you can feel it? It is hard to imagine what it feels like to know you're going to die. I know that we all have to leave this earth someday, but I don't think I'm ready for Granny to go. Life will seem so empty without her," Tammy spoke softly to Raegan in between sobs.

Raegan smiled at her. That was all she could do because she didn't have any words. She placed her arm around her friend's shoulders and squeezed tightly, hoping to reassure her that everything would be fine. Raegan had lost both of her grandmothers, so she knew exactly what Tammy was feeling. She even lost one of them to lung cancer as well. They both sat there in silence. Feeling helpless. Not knowing what to do or what to say. No power to make time stop and give Tammy her granny for years to come.

"Raegan, will you pray for my family?" Tammy requested.

"Of course I will; you know that," Raegan assured her.

"I mean, right now. Will you pray? The only comfort I know is in God's power, presence and promises," Tammy said, dabbing her wet eyes with an already tear stained napkin.

"No problem," Reagan said as she and Tammy grabbed hands, bowed their heads and closed their eyes.

"Heavenly Father, thank You for Your power and for the promises of Your Word. Thank You for Your Son Jesus who defeated death. In the name of Jesus, we come asking that You comfort Tammy's family and give them peace in the midst of their storm. We ask that You give them understanding where there is none. We ask that You begin the healing of their broken hearts right now. We believe by faith that Granny Rose will be with You when she leaves us because we believe that for the Christian to be absent from the body is to be present with the Lord. Oh, how we love You and bless Your name. We give glory to

You my God! We thank You for her life and all that she has taught. We pray that You help us to hold on to the sweet memories and times that her family had with her. In Jesus' name, we ask that her transition be pain free and that You accept Your angel back unto You. Amen."

Raegan prayed and squeezed her friend's hand and gave her another hug as she closed the prayer. She opened her eyes to find Tammy's eyes filled with more tears and Tammy's mom, cousins and brother all standing around praying with them. She empathized with them and truly hoped that they would get through the pain that they were experiencing. Raegan hugged each of them and said good-bye to give Tammy's family privacy.

CHAPTER 29

∞

While getting ready for her date with Rico, Raegan rehearsed how she would bring up the situation regarding him sending such a huge amount of money to his mother every month and how that would play into their future.

She thought it wise to also bring up the idea that they should both pull their credit reports so that they could have an open, candid discussion about finances. She hoped that this talk would go over well, but if it didn't, she felt like it would give her some indication of where their relationship was truly headed. *And an out to be with Caleb.* Perhaps this would help her see what he was all about and if he truly wanted a lasting relationship with her. She was thirty years old and she didn't want to spend time in a relationship that wasn't going anywhere. She wanted to have children someday, and based on her biological clock that day needed to be in the next few years. She didn't want to be forty years old chasing a toddler around the house.

Her rehearsal was interrupted by the sound of the doorbell ringing. He was right on time, 6:30. She went to the door, anxious. She wasn't nervous because of the date but because of what this date could mean. The conversation could possibly tear them apart. After all, she had read statistics that indicate many marriages end over financial problems; and she didn't want that to be her. Taking a deep breath, she opened the door.

"Hey babe!" she said in her sweet New York City accent. Although she was from Florida, no one would ever know it based on the way she pronounced her words. Opening the door to welcome him inside, she only needed to grab her jacket and shoes so that they could make their reservation in time.

"Thank you for being ready," Rico commented, because he usually had to wait while Raegan did *one last thing* before they went out on a date.

"You're welcome. I told you that I would try," she said with a sly wink. She grabbed her things and walked back to the door to set the alarm. "Let's go."

It was a beautiful day in November—perfect for her little black dress. Her T-strapped pumps were the icing on the cake.

"You look amazing this evening," Rico said, opening the car door for her.

"Thank you," she said, flashing a bright smile as she slid into the car. A smile that didn't quite meet her eyes because she was a little preoccupied with thoughts of Caleb. "Where are we going?"

"We're going to Three Forks. It's a very nice steakhouse downtown," Rico said as he waited for Raegan to get situated in the car.

"Sounds nice. I haven't been there before."

"Well this will be a first time for the two of us." Rico chose this restaurant because the likelihood of him seeing anyone who knew his secret was slim. The restaurant also had very dim lighting, making it easy to miss a familiar face, which is what he needed. He decided to take part of his friend's advice and be more careful about showing Raegan off all over town.

The drive into town was filled with meaningless chatter about their work weeks, plans for the holidays and different restaurants they'd tried in the area. Upon arriving at the restaurant, Rico pulled up in front of the valet stand, stepped out of his seven-year-old black Buick Regal and walked around to open the door for Raegan.

He escorted her into the restaurant, stopping short at the entrance to give the hostess his last name because he had made reservations. Raegan noted the dim lighting throughout the restaurant with beautiful paintings on the wall. Jazz music played softly in the background accompanied by soft chatter from the patrons. *Fancy,* she thought.

"Welcome. Is this your first time here?" the hostess asked. She was dressed in a black sheath dress with a gold plated name tag that read "Sheila."

"Yes, it is, for both of us," Rico said, gently rubbing his hand down Raegan's back. She had to catch herself because she nearly cringed at his touch.

What is wrong with me? She thought.

"We have some of the best steak in town and I'm not saying that because I work here," she said as she escorted them to their table. Their table was adorned with black tablecloth and tea candles. It was romantic, Raegan thought. "Here you go. Table for two. Your server will be right over to take your order. Please enjoy your dinner and your time here with us," she said, handing the menus to them as she walked away.

"Great choice. This seems like a really nice place. I hope the food tastes just as good," Raegan said, taking in the atmosphere of the restaurant.

"I agree. One of my coworkers told me about this place so I figured I would bring my future wife here to enjoy it."

"Future wife, huh? You know you keep saying that, don't you?" Raegan thought this was a perfect opportunity to bring up the issues she'd been rehearsing all evening.

"Of course, because it's true. I know we were meant to be together," Rico said with absolute certainty.

"Okay, let's talk about that a little then. Where do you see us in five years?" she started. She knew he would somehow open the door to discuss their future and now she had him right where she wanted him. She sat up straight in her seat and looked intently into his eyes. She wanted him to know that she was serious and that it was time to put his talking to the test.

"By then, we'll already be married, hopefully working on baby #2. Our careers will be going well, we'll have new cars, a big home—"

Cutting him off, she said, "All of that? What are your career plans? You know everything that you just described takes plenty of money, right?"

"Yep, when we put our money together, we're going to be ballin'," he said, making some weird gesture with his mouth.

"Okay, so let's talk about the money that you send your mom every month," she said, taking the conversation in a more serious direction. If they were seriously talking about making things work, she needed to know that he would have her best interest in mind and that she wouldn't have to worry about whether or not her and her family would be taken care of because he was sending a couple thousand dollars to his mother every month.

"What about it?" he asked slightly offended. A slight frown appeared on his face as he leaned back in his seat. He couldn't believe she was questioning him about what he did with his money.

"How much do you send her again? And how long do you plan on doing this?" she asked, eyes locked on him, waiting to hear what he was going to say. She didn't want to miss anything.

"I send her fifteen hundred dollars every month and not because I have to but because I want to. She is my mother and she has taken care of me all of her life without any help from my father, so I think she deserves that much. I don't know how long I will continue to send it to her. Why?" he asked, sounding aggravated. Although he sent money to his mother, he had other obligations in his life that had a hold on his finances. It was becoming increasingly difficult for him to live this double life.

"If we're talking about *really* being together, don't you think it's important that we talk about finances? Fifteen hundred dollars leaving our household every month is a pretty large chunk of change," she added.

"Well it may be but that's my mom," he said. His voice clearly echoed his annoyance at her line of questioning. His eyebrows wrinkled. "She is accustomed to living a certain lifestyle now; I'm not about to take that away from her. Not for you or anyone else," he said through clenched teeth.

"So how am I supposed to know that you will put the needs of our family above everyone else's? It is important to me to know that our family comes first. I'm not saying that we cannot help your mother if she needs help, but I don't think I'm comfortable with that much."

"Honestly, I didn't ask whether or not you were comfortable with it." His mood shifted.

"Let me guess. You aren't comfortable pulling your credit report either?" she asked, becoming equally agitated.

"Who said anything about that?" *She must be insane,* he thought. There was no way he was going through all of that with her. He hadn't even given her a ring. Things were good between them but she was definitely moving too fast.

"I just did. Remember, I think that we should be open about our financial information so that we won't be blindsided with financial issues after the *I dos*."

"Raegan, you can miss me with all of that nonsense." He felt like she was way out of bounds. Sure, he spoke of marrying her one day but he didn't need her in his business this way. His financial situation was just that—his. He didn't think they were anywhere near a place to be talking about things as serious as that.

Raegan was appalled. She couldn't believe he was carrying on as if talking about anything marriage related was new. He brought up the subject all the time. Leaning her head to one side and squinting her eyes, she resolved to give him a piece of her mind in the nicest way possible.

Wagging her index finger at him, she said, "Really? Five minutes ago you were talking about me being your future wife but now that I'm trying to have a serious conversation with you, I can miss you with it?" She continued without giving him a chance to speak. "Please don't go around talking about how you want to get married when you don't really want to get married. I think you just like the idea of a wife, kids and home. All of that comes with a price, dude. So how about you miss *me* with all of that marriage talk! The nerve of you," she said growing furious at the fact that she had listened to his talk for the last couple of months. *Bastard!* She thought to herself. She really wanted to use harsher words that were way outside of her character but decided against it. She knew right then and there that he wasn't worth the energy.

"I apologize. I guess I'm not ready to talk about money yet. That is a really personal subject to me," Rico said calmly, trying to restore peace between them. *Where is all of this coming from?* He wondered why she was suddenly becoming so serious, as if she had some sort of deadline.

"I know that it is and that is the reason why we really need to talk about it," she said. She started getting the feeling that he was hiding something, and with her investigative spirit, she was sure to find out just what it was.

"I understand. Can we do that later? I don't want to ruin our evening," Rico said, wanting to avoid the money conversation as much as possible. He didn't earn a ton of money and his financial situation wasn't the best, but that wasn't the reason he didn't want to talk about it. He knew that he was not in a position to marry Raegan for far greater reasons than finances and she couldn't know that.

CHAPTER 30

∞

The waitress came by a few times but they waved her off in the middle of their heated discussion. From afar, she could see that their conversation was less intense. Walking over to them, she asked if they were ready to place their order. They ordered their meals and sat quietly for a few moments. The silence became unbearable so Rico posed a question to Raegan in an attempt to lighten the mood.

"What are you going to do with your family during the holidays?"

"I can't wait," she said excitedly. "I miss them all so much. My brother is graduating from college soon, so that's exciting. I am looking forward to spending time with him. It's been a while since I last saw much of my family, so I am planning to have a great time during the week I'm there."

"Are you going to help cook?"

"Of course I am! You know I love to cook. I'll be making the dressing and oven-baked macaroni and cheese. I'm also baking the cake," said Raegan.

"Oh, that sounds delicious."

"It is. What does your family usually do," Raegan asked with a forced smile, hoping to get through the evening as quickly as possible.

"Well, it's just my mom and I, so I am going home to visit with her for a few days and then I'm heading right back to work. She usually cooks ham, dressing, greens, chitterlings and a bunch of sweets. I know that's a lot for two people but she usually gives food away to her neighbors and donates a couple of sweets to the church for the holiday dinner. Her church usually hosts a dinner for the homeless and poverty-stricken people in the area."

"That's very nice," she said as the waiter returned with their food. She had only ordered salad. After that money conversation, she didn't really want to spend much more time with him. She would find some excuse to not finish their date and have him drive her home. *He isn't really serious about a future with me*, she thought. He was starting to waste her time.

"Oh, your salad looks good."

"Thanks," she said. "Your steak looks great as well." He had a six-ounce sirloin, sweet potatoes and grilled vegetables. She did the honors of blessing the food so that they could go ahead and eat. Dinner was pretty quiet from there on out. He tried to start a conversation a few times but she was no longer interested. She couldn't believe the type of attitude he had when she wanted to discuss something serious with him. All was well when they discussed what he wanted to talk about, but not when she wanted to discuss something serious and put all of his *talking* to the test. She was so disgusted with him. There was no way he was serious about getting married, at least not as soon as he led her to believe.

Her guess was he already got what he wanted and he was using the marriage idea to keep getting it. How could she have fallen for this trickery? Wasn't this the reason that she decided to become celibate in the first place? To have a clear mind and heart when it came to relationships. To not allow anything to get in the way of her making the right decisions. To not be distracted by soul ties. Her stomach was now starting to hurt and became the perfect out for her to be able to get back home into her bed. Alone.

"My stomach is hurting, Rico. I think I'm going to have to cut this date short. I really need to get home," she said, scrunching up her face and wrapping her arms around her torso to corroborate her story.

"You don't look so well either. Is it the food?" he asked as he reached into his back pocket to pull out his wallet. He removed his credit card and placed it inside of the bill jacket that the waiter had delivered to their table. He held it in the air for a quick second to notify the waiter that he was ready to pay the bill.

The waiter quickly returned to their table, asking once more if the two would like dessert. After they responded in the negative, the waiter quickly grabbed the check and his card and left to close out their bill.

"I'm not sure, I'm just feeling a little queasy," she lied. She really only wanted to get out of his presence. She was still upset from the way he carried on earlier about the money situation. This relationship wasn't going in the direction that she had thought it was going. Part of her wanted to break it off at that very moment, but she felt as if she had invested so much of herself in such a short period of time. She had invested her body. She had been celibate for several years and she let her guard and her God down for him.

She wasn't quite sure how she had gotten to such a place, but there she was. She didn't know what to do next. Because she had given herself to him, she felt as if she needed to try to work the relationship out. She was quite sure that she wouldn't be in this place had she not slept with him, and in such a short period of time. The more she thought about it, the more she became physically ill. She really needed to get out of there and get her life together. Although she was disgusted with him, she was becoming even more disgusted with herself.

"Let's get you home then," he said. The waiter moved quickly. He had already returned with his receipt. Rico added a tip and signed the receipt. He stood from the table and reached for her hand to help her out of her seat. As they walked to the door, he noticed that the valet was already bringing his car around. The waiter had notified valet that they were getting ready to leave. *Nice service*, he thought. More restaurants should operate like this.

The ride home was pretty quiet. Raegan had an excuse to be quiet. She wasn't feeling well and he didn't want to bother her. He just wanted her to rest. She didn't know where to go from there, she realized, as she rode in silence, staring at the dark blue sky lit with a star here and there. She needed someone to talk to about all of this. Kensi or Caleb. She would have liked to talk to Caleb, but she knew that he couldn't be very objective because he wanted to be involved in a relationship with her again. She would talk to Kensi, who had nothing to gain or lose by sharing her views. She knew that Kensi's thoughts would pretty much echo her own feelings but she still needed to hear them. *Sometimes things just made more sense coming from someone else*, she thought.

"Do you need any help getting into the house?" he asked as he turned down her street.

"No, I will be fine. I'm just going to go inside and crash across my bed," she said, hoping to indicate that she would not be available to talk on the phone later that night. She was so caught up in her thoughts that she didn't even realize that they had already made it back to her subdivision.

"Alright. I will walk you to your door then," he said, pulling into her driveway. He immediately put his car in park, jumped out and quickly walked around to the passenger side of the car to open the door for her.

"Thank you," she said, reaching out her hand so that he could help her out of the car.

Rico walked her to her door and attempted to kiss her on the lips. She gave him her cheek, again using the excuse of not feeling well. He accepted it, gave her a hug and waited for her to unlock her door, enter and flip on the light before walking back to his car.

CHAPTER 31

∞

Tammy went back into her grandmother's room, where her grandmother appeared to be resting. Her mom sat at her grandmother's side, holding her hand with her head bowed.

"No, Granny," she whispered as she inched toward the bed and touched her foot. She thought her grandmother had passed away.

"Stop trying to tickle me," her grandmother said with a faint smile. Because her grandmother had lost so much weight, she could feel the slightest touch. Her body was very frail. From where she once weighed 150 pounds, she was only 89 pounds lying in that hospital bed. Her grandmother hated that her children and grandchildren had to see her that way. "Come here Tammy," her grandmother commanded.

"I'm right here," Tammy said as she moved closer to the bed and took hold of her granny's hand again.

"I need you to be strong. Your mother is going to need you baby." Her voice almost a whisper.

"Okay, I will do my best," Tammy said, trying to hold back tears. She never had anyone trying to prep her for death before.

"Baby," her grandmother said as she peered up at her with a questioning look on her face. "Are you pregnant?"

Out of all of the things her granny could have said or asked, why in the world would she ask that? "No, granny, there is nothing in this oven."

"I'm just asking. I just want to let you know that I did dream about fish and you know what that means. Somebody is pregnant or about to become pregnant."

"Well, I can assure you that it isn't me," Tammy said, smiling as she rubbed the back of her grandmother's hand.

Just then, her grandmother started to cough uncontrollably and the nurse rushed into the room at the beckon of Tammy pressing the call button. Tammy felt so helpless. She didn't know whether Granny just needed a drink of water or if she was taking her last breath. This was too much to bear! She moved out of the room with her head down. "What's wrong, Tammy?" her mother asked, quickly stepping outside behind her.

"I just don't know how to deal with this, Momma. How am I supposed to deal with this?"

"Baby, it's going to be all right, we have to accept it," her mother said, trying to convince Tammy as well as herself, while pulling her into her arms.

While they were embracing, the nurse stepped into the hallway and Tammy and her family re-entered the room.

Tammy's mom took a deep breath, arms and legs shaking, and walked into her mother's room. She walked in, along with her sisters, to tell her mother one last time that she loved her. After the brief exchange of I love yous, her mother took her last breath. The machine's steady beeps suddenly changed to one long, sad beep. The nurse walked in and turned the machine off and stood to the side, as not to interrupt. Tammy's mom moved over to the seat beside the bed, joined by her family, and sat down next to her mother for the last time and silently cried.

Although they all knew it was about to happen, it wasn't any easier to accept: Granny was no longer with them.

After consoling one another, the family parted ways, each with their own task to finalize their grandmother's memorial arrangements.

Tammy left the hospital with her mother. The drive to her mom's house was silent. They both spent the time thinking about Granny Rose, and they knew there were no words at the time that would make the situation better. When they arrived at the place where Tammy grew up, and always referred to as home, they worked at their assigned task in preparing for grandmother's homegoing services.

Once arrangements had been made and coordinated with her sisters, Tammy's mom asked, "Will you please start calling relatives to inform them that the services will take place on Saturday?"

"Yes ma'am," Tammy said, wishing she could take her mom's pain away. Just as she replied and her mom stepped out of the room, Josh called. She went back and forth with herself about whether or not she should answer, but decided that she would, hoping that it would lift her spirits just a bit. She stepped out of the house for a moment to take the call.

"Hey there," she said, with an attempt to mask her sadness. She pulled her sweater tighter as she slowly paced back and forth in the front yard.

"Hey Tammy." He could tell by the way her voice sounded that something was wrong. When she explained what happened, he said, "I'm so sorry Tammy, I'll be there on the first available flight out on tomorrow."

"You don't have to do that, but it will mean a lot to me if you can make it to the services on Saturday. I think Granny would have wanted that."

"Consider it done. I will arrive on Thursday to help out with anything that needs to be done."

"Thanks, Josh," she said, smiling and thankful.

"No problem. Please call me in the meantime if you need anything. I mean that."

"That means a lot to me Josh...I have to go help my mom now, so I will talk with you later," she said, bringing the conversation to an end.

"Okay. I will touch base with you later in the week," he said, reluctantly ending the call. He wanted to call her later that day and talk with her as much as he could, but he didn't want to push her. He also knew that now probably wasn't the best time with the recent passing of her grandmother.

"Thanks. I will talk to you then. Bye sweetheart," Tammy said, ending the call. She held the phone to her chest and closed her eyes for a moment. She said a quick prayer for her family, especially her mother, and went back inside the house to start calling family with the details of Granny's memorial services.

CHAPTER 32

∞

The service was beautiful, though Tammy didn't like the viewing of the body before the service. The person lying in that casket looked nothing like her Granny. It was just a lifeless body covered with make-up and clothes that was supposed to be her. Granny would never wear all of that make-up, but she understood that they were trying to make Granny look her best. Her mother made sure that Granny was wearing a pretty dress in her favorite color—purple.

A few friends and family members paid tribute to Granny when asked if anyone had anything they wanted to share. At a time when she wanted to cry, she laughed. One of her cousins stood at the mic saying stuff that didn't make any sense at all. It was so funny and caused everyone else to giggle a little bit too. She may not have been trying to lighten the mood but she really did. One of her aunts sang

Granny's favorite song; another cousin wrote and read a poem. It was all very touching.

After the service, they went to the gravesite to pray one last time before her body was lowered into the dark, deep hole in the ground. Tammy was happy to have Joshua, Raegan, Michelle and Kensi there to support her and her family. After leaving the gravesite, they went back to the fellowship hall of the church for the repast. The mood lightened a bit as they shared food and stories about her grandmother. Granny would have been happy to know that all of her family had come together to celebrate her. They hadn't had a family reunion in about sixteen years. Tammy thought that it would be a good idea to talk with her mom about planning a reunion sometime over the next year or two. She didn't want the only time they came together to be weddings and funerals. She was sure that her grandma would have wanted this and that it was good for the family as well.

When the weekend ended, and everyone returned home, Joshua stayed behind. He felt that Tammy needed him and he did not want to abandon her at a time like this. Besides, it was holiday season and he wanted to make sure her memories for holiday seasons to come weren't all sad thoughts.

Tammy took advantage of having Joshua around for a little while longer. She released her feelings and he enjoyed being a listening ear. Joshua took advantage of any additional time that he could get with her as well. He helped clean her grandmother's home, ran errands for her mother and even cooked dinner a few times. Tammy's mother was very appreciative because she was still having a difficult time, although things were getting better. It helped to have someone around to pick up the slack.

In order to lift Tammy's spirits even more, Joshua asked Tammy out to dinner one night, after cooking dinner for her mother and brother. He wanted her to see him as more than just an estranged husband who was there for her in her time of need. He wanted her to begin seeing some type of future with him again.

"Tammy, I have to leave town to get back for my game, but I'd like to spend some time alone with you before I leave, if you're okay with that," he said as he walked over next to her, his tall frame towering over her.

"That's fine. What do you have in mind?" she asked, looking up at him. She actually needed time away to breathe fresh air and to take her mind off of her loss and all of the sadness.

"I made dinner for your mom and brother but I'd like to take you out so that we can talk. Is that all right with you?"

"Okay, where do you want to go?" she asked slowly, thinking that he must already have a plan.

"I'll let you choose."

"Hmmm…Let's go to Pappadeaux. I love their shrimp, boudain and crabfingers. I have a taste for that right about now."

"I'm ready when you're ready," Joshua said, grateful that they were going to get some time alone.

Getting hungrier just thinking about it, she said, "I'm ready now. Let me first tell my mom that I'm stepping out with you for a while and check to see if she needs anything." Tammy went to the kitchen to find her mom and brother preparing their plates to eat the baked chicken, baked macaroni and cheese and green beans that Joshua had cooked. "Hey guys, I'm going to go out with Joshua for a while. Do you need anything before we leave?" she asked. Her mom looked at her brother as he shook his head no while scarfing down the food.

"We're okay baby. Have a good time," her mom said with a wink.

"All right. See you all in a few," Tammy said, shaking her head at her mom. She was just like Granny when it came to Josh. They had always rooted for Joshua and something told Tammy that her mom was still in his corner. *It's just dinner,* she thought. No one, including her mother, agreed with her decision to give up on her marriage, so even the smallest hope that the two of them would get back together brought a smile to her mom's eyes.

Tammy grabbed her jacket and walked back into the living room to find Joshua flipping through a photo album on the coffee table. All of her childhood photos were in there.

"I'm ready," she said as she reached for the photo album. "What about you?"

"You were a beautiful little girl with your braces," he said, giving her a compliment but also teasing her.

"Yeah, yeah. I know. Let's go."

Joshua grabbed his jacket from the coat rack near the front door, opened the door for her and walked to his rental car. As they walked down the brick walkway lined with beautiful tulips, he quickly stepped ahead of her so that he could open her car door. After making sure she was in safely, he hopped into the car and turned on the ignition. He smiled as the sweet sounds of music captured his attention.

"Do you know this song?"

"Yes, I like Elliot Yamin," she said as his song, "Wait for You" played. She thought she was hearing the radio but it was actually Joshua's iPod. He wanted her to hear the song because he was slowly trying to send the message that he wanted to be with her and that he would wait until she was ready to give their marriage a chance again.

"I do as well. I like most of his music," he said while searching for the restaurant in his GPS. Moments later, he put the car in reverse, backed out of the driveway and began the journey to the restaurant.

"You still enjoy shrimp, huh?"

"Definitely! As long as they aren't cocktail shrimp. I don't know who came up with that idea. Cocktail shrimp are disgusting. Yuck," she said, frowning at the thought of cold shrimp. The ride to the restaurant continued on with conversation about their love for seafood. That was one thing they both had in common: their love for seafood, actually food in general.

Upon arrival to Pappadeaux, they were quickly seated. It was the middle of the week and there was no crowd. For that, they were thankful because they were hungry. They didn't want to fill up on the bread. Tammy was also grateful that the hostess recognized Joshua and seated them in a booth in the rear of the restaurant to help reduce any unwanted attention.

Tammy was glad that she had remembered her jacket. Even though it wasn't chilly outside, it was still cool in the restaurant. She glanced at the menu to make sure she had the name of the entrée correct because she already had in mind what she wanted to order. Joshua took a couple of minutes and when he finished, he placed the menu in front of him as to signal to the waitress that they were ready. They ordered their food at the same time they placed their drink order. They didn't want to prolong dinner any longer than they had to.

"How are you feeling Tammy? I know that may sound like a silly question but really, I want to know," he said, his deep tenor voice interrupting her thoughts of food.

"I'm getting better. I knew Granny was sick and that she would eventually leave us. I guess I'm more worried about Momma. She was Granny's youngest child and she spent the most time with her in her last days. I just want her to be all right without making her feel like I'm sticking around to keep an eye on her or out of pity. I know that we all have to grieve but I just want to make sure she's okay."

"I understand," he said reaching for one of her hands. "I know how hard this is for you and how close you were to your grandmother. Even though I have to return to Boston, I want you to call me anytime you need to talk or if you need me here," he said, staring into her eyes. He wanted her to know that he was serious about giving her what she needed from him.

"Thanks, Josh. I really appreciate you being here for me and my family over the last week. I know my mom really appreciates all that you've done to help out, and so do I. Granny would be happy," she said, smiling as she thought of her granny.

"I'm happy to help out. They're still my family too. There was no way I could live with myself if I hadn't been here to chip in."

"I owe you one..."

"You don't. However, if you want to owe me, I know exactly how you can repay me."

"And how is that?" she questioned him, already having an idea of what his answer would be.

"Say you'll come to Boston to visit me again or allow me to come here to visit you. I know the season is about to pick up, but we can work something out. Just say you'll agree to it," he said cornering her. She brought it upon herself but the more she thought about it, the more she liked the idea of seeing more of him.

"Okay. I suppose we can work something out." She winked at him, removing the lemon from her water and taking a sip.

"That's my girl," he said, raising his fist to hers to give her a pound. He always did that when he got his way. She laughed at him and met his fist with hers. Just as they finished the gesture, their waitress returned to their table with their food.

"Oh, this looks delicious!" she said, anxious to begin her meal.

"Ummm," he said in agreement, grabbed her hand once more and blessed the food.

"Can I try yours?" she asked before he could even try it himself.

"Sure, as long as you let me try one of those shrimp," he said teasing. He knew how much she loved shrimp and didn't like to share.

"Okay," she said as she cut a very small piece off one of her shrimp so that he could taste it.

"Tammy, that's cold," he said chuckling, "but I'll accept that this time."

"What? I only have about six shrimp over here. Show a little mercy," she said, trying to justify her selfish actions when it came to her food.

"Uh huh," he said opening his mouth so that she could feed it to him. "This is pretty good. Great choice!"

"Thanks," she said, parting her lips so that he could feed her a piece of his grilled mahi mahi. "Oh my goodness, it is melting in my mouth. Excellent!"

They continued to chat about food, their schedules and families throughout dinner. They made plans to visit with each other once per month during basketball season. Joshua was happy about that. He felt like he was another step closer to getting his wife back. He just needed to take care of a few things back in Boston. He was seeing someone but it wasn't serious. However, he needed to end things with her because he wanted nothing getting in the way of him making things right again with Tammy.

CHAPTER 33

∞

On the drive home, Rico began to feel as if there had been a change in their relationship. He loved Raegan and wanted to marry her, but the reality of that set in when she wanted to discuss his financial situation. That conversation completely caught him off guard and he didn't know what to make of it. It's not as if he had already proposed, so why did she want to get so serious all of a sudden? Up to this point, their relationship had been fun and he enjoyed the time that they were spending together. On many occasions, he had mentioned that he wanted to marry her, and he did, but not tomorrow. He couldn't even if he wanted to. He wasn't anywhere close to being the man that he wanted to be in any aspect: mentally, emotionally, spiritually or free of attachments.

He was well aware that he had a lot of growing to do, and he thought that Raegan could see and understand that. However, he knew that Raegan came from a home where her mother and father had been married for many years. She saw them work through so many things together and felt like they could work through anything together as well. But he wasn't her father and she wasn't her mother. He wasn't ready for all of that.

Rolling the window down and allowing the cool air to hit his face, he continued to think about all that transpired between the two of them tonight. The more he thought about their relationship and the kind of lady Raegan was, the more he knew that he had to break up with her. She was obviously more mature and had thought about this thing way more than he had. He had to be honest with himself. He couldn't be the kind of man she wanted or needed him to be. The challenge now became how he would end things with her. He would have to come up with something; he couldn't tell her the truth, or she would hate him forever.

His thoughts were interrupted by a call from his *wife*. He was glad that he had already dropped Raegan off at home. He was surprised to receive a call from his wife because she was supposed to be working all weekend. She was a nurse at Veterans Memorial Hospital. She often worked long hours and most weekends, so she had no idea what he was up to most of the time.

"Hey sweetheart!" he said as he answered the phone. "I was just thinking about you."

"I was thinking of you too; that's why I called. It sounds like you're in the car. Where are you headed?"

"I'm heading back home. I just stepped out to get some Chinese takeout. Why don't you come home and enjoy some of this takeout and good lovin'?"

"Oh, honey, I wish I could. I have more rounds to do but I'm going to take off next weekend so that we can spend some time together. I miss you so much and I know that we haven't had much time together lately. I'll even do that little thing you like."

"All right girl, don't make me come up there and meet you in the on-call room," he said. *Where did that come from? Too much Greys Anatomy with Raegan,* he thought. That thought alone confirmed that he needed to do something about his relationship with Raegan. She was interfering in his marriage in ways he hadn't expected.

"I'm sure you would," she said, glancing at her watch. "I have to go, I love you honey. Have a good night and enjoy that takeout. That sounds so good right about now."

"I love you too," he said. Even though he had just eaten, Chinese did sound good at that time. He decided to make part of his lie the truth and found a Chinese restaurant to purchase takeout for his wife to eat during her lunch break that night. He figured he would surprise her. He knew that he wasn't being the best husband and could try a little harder, so he considered that to be his first step in being a better spouse.

CHAPTER 34

∞

Meanwhile, back at home, Raegan called Kensi to discuss her intense conversation with Rico concerning finances. Even talking about it made her stomach hurt. She repeated the entire exchange to Kensi almost verbatim, giving her commentary on his responses to her questions.

What bothered Raegan the most was that Rico acted like she offended him when he was the one who brought up this whole subject of marriage in the first place. It's not as if Raegan had been pressuring him, but after tonight's argument, she got the feeling that he felt like she was.

"This whole situation just sounds off Rae. I'm telling you, he is hiding something. It is up to you to find out what it is or if you think it's even worth it to stick around and find out."

"Yeah, I know. At this point, I don't even think it's worth it," Raegan said. She was curled up in bed because the entire situation had her feeling physically ill.

"I mean what I'm about to say in the nicest way possible. He doesn't want to marry you, honey. He may think that he does but he doesn't. Any man serious about getting married wouldn't act like that."

"You're probably right. What—" Raegan was interrupted by a beep on her phone. It was Caleb, a rainbow in the middle of her storm. "Hey Kensi, I have a call. Let me take this and I will give you a call tomorrow."

"Okay, tell Caleb I said hi. Before you deny it, I already know that no one else is going to be calling you at this time of night. Your mother is in bed. Goodnight," she said laughing as she ended the call.

"Bye girl." Switching to the other line, she answered, "Hey Caleb, what's up?" His voice was just what she needed to hear after that fiasco with Rico earlier that night. Luckily for her, Caleb was returning to town the next day to do some house hunting. He had already been in touch with a realtor and found a few houses to check out. His current objective was to talk Raegan into joining him on the house tours.

"Hey, I'm halfway sorry for calling you so late, but I wanted to remind you that I'll be in town tomorrow."

"Sure, you're sorry," she said checking the time, noticing that it was now 10:08 p.m.

"You're right, not really. I'm glad you're still awake. Will you be available after church in the morning? I could really use your opinion tomorrow. I'm going to be touring new homes with my realtor, Teresa. Can you come out? Please?" he asked. She could imagine his dark, engaging eyes pleading with her, making it hard for her to turn him down, although at this point she didn't want to say no anyway.

"I love looking at new homes; I'll come out for a little while. Do you know how many homes you're going to look at while you're here?"

"We're planning to see five tomorrow. If nothing comes of that, I will choose a few more during my next visit. I don't want to spend all of my time looking for a place; I want to save some of that time reconnecting with you, Cami," he said. He wanted to make it clear that what he wanted most was her.

She loved how direct he could be when stating what he wanted. She missed that and had thought she had found that in Rico, but he didn't know what he wanted, she concluded. She didn't want to waste time thinking of him either, so she switched her thoughts back to Caleb.

"I'm sure I can squeeze you in. What time does your plane land? Do you need a ride from the airport or are you renting a car?"

"My plane lands at 8 a.m. I'm going to rent a car, so you don't have to pick me up from the airport. That was sweet of you to offer though," he said. She could feel his smile through the phone.

"Actually, I didn't offer."

"You did. Are you going to church in the morning? I'd like to tag along if you don't mind. I'll need to find a new church home as well. I can start with yours." He was not going to miss out on any chance to be with her.

"Sure, we'd love to have you. Service starts at 9:30 though, so you'll likely need to head straight to church when you leave the airport. You will probably arrive in just enough time."

"Sounds like a plan to me. I'll let you get your beauty rest. I have to finish packing and get some rest myself. I have an early flight in the morning."

"Have a good night. I shall see you in service tomorrow," she smiled as she chewed her bottom lip. She was looking forward to his visit just as much as he was.

"Good night beautiful. Dream about me," he said as he ended the call. He didn't need to tell her that; she would be dreaming about him anyway. In fact, she hadn't stopped dreaming about him since she laid eyes on him during her girls' weekend a couple of years ago.

Caleb was glad that he didn't have to do much pleading with Raegan to get her to come house hunting with him. Before things went sour, they had such a great relationship. He was hoping to rekindle that soon, and the house that she helped him pick would soon be their new home. He felt like they were mature enough adults who knew what they wanted. He would make his intentions toward her clear because they had spent a lot of time apart; however, he wanted her to know that he had every intention of making her Mrs. Caleb McKinney.

Back at home, Raegan settled into her bed feeling many different emotions: anxiety, anger, happiness, confusion, sadness, enthusiasm and fear. She was on an emotional roller-coaster. From being totally excited about Rico to being confused and angry, she didn't know what to think about her relationship with him, if there was anything left of it.

And then there was Caleb. From never wanting to hear from him or see him again to being excited about hearing his voice on the phone and looking forward to spending time with him, she wondered where her life was going. Her friends often considered her to be the one who had it all together. Looking at her life now, that couldn't be further from the truth. She felt like she needed to make some decisions to straighten things out, but she just didn't know what decisions to make or even how to make them. She hoped that tomorrow's sermon was going to be one of those that were just for her.

Raegan tried as hard as she could to dismiss her thoughts and settle into sleep. She settled into her king-sized canopy bed, fit for a queen, pulled her green jacquard comforter up to her chin, rolled over to her left side and dozed off. After finding sleep, her thoughts resumed turning. She dreamed that she was on a ship in the middle of the ocean, caught in a terrible storm. The ship was being tossed about as if it was going to turn over. No one else was on the ship but her. She was becoming so terrified that she woke up in a cold sweat, fearing what was going to happen to her. She got out of bed and walked into the kitchen to drink a half glass of water. After shaking the dream off, she headed back to bed to get some rest before church in the morning.

Raegan woke up the next morning remembering the terrible dream she had. It didn't return when she fell asleep the second time, but she did remember it and it bothered her. She didn't know what it meant but she felt like it was a warning of something terrible about to happen. In an effort to remove the thoughts from her mind, she turned on her inspirational music and stepped into the shower.

On cue, when she finished her shower, Caleb called to let her know that his plane had just landed. He also asked if she would wait for him before finding a seat so that they could sit together. He wanted to sit beside someone he knew. She agreed and ended the call. She hadn't found anything to wear the night before so she had to spend a few moments going through her closet. She stepped into her walk-in closet and began pulling clothes off the hangers to try on. After trying on several dresses, she decided on a gray knee-length pencil skirt with a split in the back and a silk purple top. Still inside the closet, she stepped over to her full-length mirror to make sure that she looked appropriate for church. She often wore that skirt to work but depending on how her weight was acting that day, it could be slightly inappropriate for church. Satisfied that she looked good, she put the other items back on the hangers, switched off the lights and walked out of the closet. She walked back into the restroom in her master suite to touch up her signature beautiful curls. She wanted to make sure that she looked great today since she was going to spend a lot of time with Caleb.

She was excited about Caleb attending church with her but she wasn't too thrilled about the whispers that would be going on because of it. Church folks were nosey and even when you thought they weren't paying attention, they were. It didn't really matter who you were. *Oh well,* she thought. *Who cares?* She was a grown woman finally becoming comfortable in her own skin; she didn't care what other people thought.

She looked at the clock and noticed that she only had about fifteen more minutes before she needed to leave the house. She had spent way too much time trying to find something to wear. She only had a few minutes for breakfast if she wanted to make it to church on time. She walked barefooted into the kitchen on the cold tile floor and opened the refrigerator door, staring inside for a few seconds trying to decide what she should eat. She decided on eggs and toast. She grabbed her ingredients and quickly scrambled two eggs and prepared cinnamon toast. As she sat down to eat at her breakfast nook, she noticed a text from Rico asking if she felt better. She ignored it. She didn't feel like responding. She was still pretty upset with him.

After her quick breakfast, she slipped on her shoes and coat, grabbed her purse and headed to her car in the garage to leave. She was feeling pretty good about seeing Caleb today; it just felt right. She didn't want to get too excited though and decided to let things happen as they should.

Arriving at the church, she noticed Caleb walking across the parking lot on his way to the entrance. She pulled up beside him, let down her window and said, "Good morning, handsome."

He knew that voice anywhere. He quickly turned around and said, "Good morning, beautiful." He looked great that morning. He was dressed in a heather gray suit, white crisp shirt and purple tie. They were color coordinated.

"Hey, let me find a parking space and I will meet you right here," she said.

"I don't mind waiting," he said, stepping back out of the parking lot so that she could drive away and find a parking space.

They were attending the early service, so it wasn't difficult for Raegan to find a space. After parking, she quickly grabbed her purse and Bible, did one final mirror check and stepped out of her coupe. She wasn't far away from where he was standing so he watched her as she walked toward him, drinking in her beauty. He was excited about spending time with her today and had high hopes of spending as much time with her as possible while he was in town this week.

"Well aren't you a ray of sunshine this morning?" he said while giving her elevator eyes. He couldn't stop looking at her. She was the only woman who kept his attention and was looking forward to being the only man who did the same for her.

"If that means you think I look great, then thank you," she said, flirting with him as well. "You look handsome this morning. I'm glad that you were able to make it." He smiled at her response as they walked into the building to enter the sanctuary.

The worship service seemed to start and end quickly. When it was over, she felt as if she'd just got there, but she didn't miss the message and it was exactly what she needed to hear that morning. The pastor talked about God revealing things to us and how we need to have the wisdom and courage to act upon it. She applied that to her life and knew that she needed to do something. But she wasn't quite sure she had all the courage she needed just yet. She didn't want Caleb to be the reason that she decided to end things with Rico. She wanted to be absolutely sure that things couldn't go any further.

<u>CHAPTER 35</u>

∞

"Let's take advantage of the extra time we have before meeting my realtor. Have brunch with me, Cami," Caleb said. It was more of a statement than a question.

"I'd like that. Where would you like to go?" Raegan responded. She was glad that he joined her for church. She enjoyed all of her time with him, and wanted it to continue, with not one thought of her withering relationship with Rico.

"How about we take your car home first so that we can travel together, and then we can decide on some place to eat. Does that work for you?"

"That's fine," she said. Spending time with Caleb was definitely not going to help her sort through her relationship troubles with Rico, but that didn't matter to her.

After saying hello to some of her fellow church members and introducing them to Caleb, they said their good-byes and walked to the parking lot. Caleb walked her to her car, opened the door for her, helped her inside and walked around to his Jeep rental. He was only parked two spaces away from her. He then followed her home and waited for her to come out of the garage to get into the car with him. Before she made it to his car, he was already standing next to the passenger door, waiting to open it for her and help her inside. He treated her like she was a delicate piece of china and she loved every moment of it. She was never going to be able to keep a clear head with all of this going on, she thought.

In the car, they decided to have brunch at Mia Bella's. The atmosphere was quiet, the food was pretty good and it wasn't very far away; they would have plenty of time to get to know each other again. After arriving at the restaurant and being seated, they immediately began chatting away about that morning's sermon and the house hunting ahead. As they talked, she rubbed her stocking-clad foot up against his pants leg. She was so engaged in the conversation that she didn't even realize that she was doing it. They were both so engrossed in the conversation that they didn't notice the waitress.

"You two look nice this morning with your purple and gray. You make such a gorgeous couple," the waitress commented.

Before Raegan could interject, Caleb thanked the waitress and asked for a few more minutes to scan the menu before placing their orders. They spent a few moments glancing through the lively gold menus.

Everything looked so delicious from omelets to French toast, Belgian waffles and potatoes. They decided on different items so that they could try each other's food. Caleb signaled for the waitress to return so that they could place their orders.

When the waitress left, he said, "You can continue doing that little thing you were doing with your foot."

She was a little caught off guard and embarrassed. All she could say was "okay," although she didn't continue. She didn't realize she was doing that and was grateful that the waitress didn't take very long to return with their food. Perfect timing. Caleb took a moment to bless the food and she needed that moment to recollect herself.

"You know you're going to be the only friend I'm going to have out here when I move, so I'm going to need a lot of companionship," he said, winking at her.

"Work should keep you busy and I'm sure you can find company quickly. You're a great catch," she said, twirling her fork to emphasize her point.

"That may be true but I'm not looking for other company. All the company I need is sitting right in front of me, eating eggs and caressing my leg with her foot," he said rather directly.

"I see," she said, taking a sip of her mimosa. She didn't have much else to say to that. Thinking of a way to switch the subject, she checked the time. It was about time for them to leave and get started on the house hunting. "I think we should be preparing to leave so that you can make your first appointment on time," she said, pointing to her diamond bracelet watch.

He checked the time and agreed. He raised his hand once more to signal for the waitress to come attend to their table. When the waitress arrived, he asked her for the check. When she walked away, he began to speak once more.

"I noticed that you didn't say much when I mentioned I wanted to spend my free time with you when I move to town. I'm serious about us repairing our relationship and moving forward together, Cami. I want you to understand that. I don't know what business you have going on with Rico, and honestly, I don't care. I know that it won't last much longer anyway, so just let me know when you're ready for your future," he said, reaching into his wallet for his credit card to pay for the check.

"Wow." She chuckled a little. "Just like that huh? So you're my future?" she asked, resting back in her chair to focus on his beautiful, almond-shaped brown eyes. She thought that his eyes and chiseled jaw line were his most handsome features.

"Yes. I am very clear about my intentions with you and what I want in life. I have had my share of wild and crazy times, so I'm not looking for that type of life. I want the house, wife, children, kids' softball games, dance recitals and everything that comes along with that. Most importantly, I want that with you. No one else," he said, not batting an eye.

As he spoke, her heart fluttered. Now why didn't Rico just say all of that a few nights ago? But who cares now? He was practically out the door and she was actually glad that he didn't say that. If he did, she probably wouldn't be sitting there with the love of her life right now. She just didn't know how she was going to get to that place with Caleb when Rico was, in fact, still in the picture. As disgusted as she was with him, and herself, she didn't want to break his heart. There had to be a way that everyone could win in all of this. She would just need to figure out how.

After Caleb paid the check, he stood up and walked around to her seat to help her out of her chair. Their fingers immediately intertwined as they walked across the restaurant towards the door. When they arrived at his car, he didn't miss a beat. He continued to be a gentleman by opening her car door, helping her inside.

When he slid into the Jeep, he continued his conversation about his intentions toward her. "Cami, based on my confession about my intentions moments ago, you do know why I want you to come along with me now, don't you?"

"Why don't you just tell me?" she asked. She wanted to hear the words coming from his lips. She'd rather not assume anything.

Before turning on the ignition, he shifted in his seat to face her and answered her question. "You're about to choose your future home. I want you to be able to see yourself living in the house that I buy. I want you to be able to see yourself raising our children in this house."

"You are pretty confident. You are aware that I now own the house that I like, right?" she asked, her body now turned in his direction.

"I know you own a house and we can work out all of those details later. Remember that I'm your future," He said, leaning forward to kiss her softly on the lips. The warmth of his lips against hers caused her to feel something she hadn't felt in a long time. Sparks. Butterflies.

"I hear you," she said, slowly pulling away. Again, she didn't know how to respond to that. She knew that he wanted to be involved with her, but that kiss caught her off guard, although she welcomed it.

"That's all I am asking. That you hear me and understand what my intentions are regarding us," he said, satisfied that he was getting through to her. And if that kiss was any indication, she felt the same way.

He put the address into the navigation system and drove to the first house. It was about ten miles away. When they pulled up to the home, they couldn't help but notice the immaculate landscaping. It was quite evident that there was newly planted grass. Beautiful purple and red flowers lined both sides of the sidewalk. A beautiful fruit tree grew near the side of the house, surrounded by fresh mulch. A gorgeous swing with brown, cream and red striped pillows adorned the front porch between two tall columns. Walking up the sidewalk to the front of the house, she noticed the double door frames with glass panels surrounded by the house brick.

"I love what I see already," she said, taking in the beautiful landscaping.

"I am enjoying the view as well," he agreed as they walked toward the door hand in hand. The front door opened just as they were about to knock. His realtor stood smiling in the doorway.

"Do you like what you see so far?" she asked, taking note of their facial expressions.

"Yes!" they said in unison.

"Great! Come inside to take a look at the rest. I will hang around downstairs to give you two a chance to look at the entire house. When you're done, come back down to meet me in the kitchen."

"Sounds good. Thanks," said Caleb. He was grateful that she allowed them to tour the home without standing over their shoulders trying to sell it to them. He often found that distracting and just wanted the chance to see if they could visualize themselves living there.

They continued to walk through the home in awe. The home was about 3,500 square feet. Raegan thought that it was too much space but very lovely. All the countertops were granite. Every appliance in the kitchen was stainless steel. There was a huge island in the middle of the kitchen. Plenty of cabinet space. A formal dining area and a breakfast nook. The master suite was gorgeous with double closets, double sinks and double showers and a jetted whirlpool spa tub. To Raegan, the only thing that mattered in any home was the kitchen; everything else was just another room. Noting the beauty of the home, they went downstairs to talk to the realtor.

"So, what did you all think?" she asked excitedly, clasping her hands together.

"Cami, why don't you tell me what you liked about it," he said, making it clear that her opinion mattered most to him.

"I didn't know you were going to put me on the spot like that, but I'd have to say that the kitchen and master suite are both absolutely gorgeous. Overall, I think this may be too much house but I like it," said Raegan.

"I think you two forgot something. You didn't check out the backyard," the realtor said with a huge grin, pointing over her shoulder with her thumbs. She hoped that the backyard would be the selling point. The backyard was huge and completely finished with an outdoor kitchen, enclosed covered patio, gazebo about a hundred feet away from the back door and enough room for a children's swing set.

Raegan turned to look at Caleb. "Do you see this?" she asked, her eyes widened. "This is unbelievable! I love it!" Raegan twirled around the patio, touching the cooking appliances and countertops.

Laughing and comforted by her enthusiasm, he responded by saying, "Yes, it is gorgeous. So what do you think? Do you want it?" He stood there with his hands in his pockets gazing at her intently. He would buy the house today if he knew it would make her happy.

She had gotten swept away in the moment, forgetting about all the troubles that lay ahead of her. She did, in fact, want that house. The backyard was great for entertaining and children's activities and she was absolutely in love with the kitchen and master suite.

"I don't know," she said smiling as she tapped her chin with an index finger. "I think we should still look at other options, but this one is definitely a contender," Raegan said.

Walking back inside and turning to his realtor, Caleb said, "The lady loves it, but we still want to look at others before making a final decision. Maybe something a little smaller with the same great features."

"I have just the house. We can ride together or you two can meet me there. It is okay to leave your car here."

"Sure, we can ride with you," Caleb said, glancing at Raegan to see if she was okay with it.

Raegan nodded and smiled, walking closer to Caleb to grab his hand, completely lost in the moment. Holding his hand, she knew that is where she was meant to be.

They spent the rest of the afternoon looking at houses, but none measured up to the first house. The houses were either too small or weren't comparable to the asking price. The two of them were both in agreement that the first house was the most stunning. On the ride back to the first home, they discussed whether or not Caleb should look at more houses on his next visit or whether he should put in a bid on the first house. He told his realtor that he would talk it over in detail with Raegan and give her an answer before he returned to Georgia. She agreed that was a good idea and that he shouldn't make any hasty decisions. They decided to take another look at the first house, since they were there, to relish in its beauty before going home.

"That has to be one of the most amazing houses that I've ever seen," Raegan said to Caleb as he helped her back into the Jeep.

Back into the driver's side and starting the engine, he said, "I have to agree with you. I wasn't expecting anything like that. Do you want to talk about it over dinner? It's been several hours since brunch now and I'm hungry again." He was hoping to convince her to stay out with him a little bit longer.

"I think I can eat again, but I have a taste for Chinese. I know this really great Chinese restaurant that we can go to, but it is about twenty-five miles away. Are you okay with that?"

Caleb answered affirmatively. He was grateful for any extra time that he could have with her. They had been apart for far too many years; he didn't want to miss out on any opportunity to win her heart back.

CHAPTER 36

∞

Back in Boston, Tammy was enjoying the company of Joshua. As promised, he returned to see her a few weeks after her grandmother's funeral. Now it was her turn to visit him and he had made sure nothing would get in the way. He took care of her travel arrangements for the current visit and her subsequent visit. She knew that Granny would be happy that they were trying to work things out.

Joshua was working really hard to prove to Tammy that she would not have to compete with his career but that he would put her first. He also encouraged her to be more patient and to understand the type of career that he had. Because he was an athlete, an MVP at that, he would have to practice and travel very often. He didn't see any reason why they couldn't be together because of it, but she was still hesitant. He hadn't thought it was an issue when they wed in college, but Tammy did. She believed that as newlyweds, they should be focused on each other and that he wasn't prioritizing his time very well. She didn't really understand how things worked in the NBA. However, he now felt like it was his duty to help her understand so that she could become a part of his life again.

"Hey, was that your mom on the phone?" Josh asked Tammy as he kissed her on the cheek. She was sitting at a barstool in front of the kitchen island sipping hot cocoa.

"No, it was Raegan. We didn't talk long, but I get the feeling that something is up with her."

"Is that right? What do you think it could be?" he asked as he took a seat next to her, grabbing his mug of cocoa and taking a sip. "This is some good stuff. What did you do to it? This isn't just some packaged cocoa mix. What's the secret?"

"Nah, can't tell you," she said, shaking her head and showing her thinly gapped tooth smile. "I can't quite put my finger on what's up with Raegan but I know it's relationship related. You know how you guys always have us about to lose our minds with your shenanigans. I will find out sooner or later though."

"She will tell you when the time is right. Don't worry about it. If she isn't telling you something, I'm sure she has her reasons. Don't you think?" he asked, scooting away from her to stand up from the barstool.

"Now about this hot cocoa recipe, since you won't give me the recipe, does that mean you'll just be making it for me every winter?"

"You expect me to fly out here just to make hot cocoa for you?" Tammy asked confused. "I don't think so."

"Well, you don't have to fly out here; you can just wake up and make it, make it when you come home from work, make it when we're sitting down to have a conversation and relax. It doesn't really matter, as long as you agree to make it every winter," he said, pulling a little blue box out of his Nike tear-away pants pocket and simultaneously getting down on one knee.

"Oh my!?" she whispered through the tears forming in her eyes.

"What do you say? Will you make hot chocolate for me every winter? Will you be my wife again, Tammy?" Joshua asked as he opened the blue box, showcasing a three carat princess cut diamond ring. She still had the first engagement ring he gave to her but he wanted to give her a new one as a symbol that they were leaving the past behind them and starting over.

"Yes, I'll be your wife and make my special hot cocoa for you whenever you want!" she exclaimed, nodding her head. They had talked about the possibility of getting back together but she didn't know that he would be asking her so soon. Her granny would be so happy and she knew that it would brighten her mom's day. She couldn't wait to share the news with her family and friends.

He placed the ring on her finger. It was gorgeous. She wished that her nail polish wasn't chipped but the ring was so gorgeous, anyone looking at her hand wouldn't even notice her unkempt nails.

*****

The next day Joshua had a game. Because she was his special guest, she had a floor seat. When she arrived at her seat, she saw familiar faces waiting to greet her—her mom and brother! Josh flew them into town to keep her company during the game. For that, she was grateful.

The game was going really well and their team was up by twenty-two points. It was an exciting game until the third quarter. Joshua had the ball. He was running circles around the other team when he went up for a slam dunk and came crashing down to the floor. The referee blew the whistle to halt the game because Joshua did not get up off the floor. In fact, he wasn't moving at all. The emergency team rushed to his side to check on him. They moved his body to a gurney and lifted him away from the floor.

"No!" she screamed, running onto the floor, breaking all kinds of rules. *This could not be happening just as things were starting to go well with them,* she thought. The referees tried to usher her back to her seat but she was adamant about being by his side. After she screamed numerous times that she is his wife and she wasn't going anywhere, they relented. "Joshua, honey, can you hear me?" she asked, her hands trembling as she kneeled at his side. He remained unresponsive.

Joshua was airlifted to the hospital. She rode along with him but the car she arrived in took her family to the hospital where they were taking him.

When Joshua and Tammy arrived at the hospital, he was whisked away to receive emergency care. However, she was furious because no one would tell her anything or allow her to see him. All she could do was pace the floor in the waiting area, waiting, hoping and praying that good news would come soon.

She looked up for a moment and noticed the doctor speaking to a beautiful young woman who was dressed in a black pants suit with patent leather heels. She overheard the woman inquiring about his condition. She immediately walked over to the doctor and the woman. "Excuse me, I'm Tammy, Joshua's wife. Who are you?" Tammy was surprised at how calm she sounded because she wanted to scream. Why was there another woman at the hospital asking about his condition? And why was the doctor talking to her?

"Wife? Oh, yes, he told me about you. I'm Megan Smart, his attorney," she said, extending her hand to Tammy but she refused. His attorney then reached into her briefcase. "I have some documents for you to look over and sign. Please come have a seat with me for a moment, if you don't mind."

"Wait, what? Of course I mind! You're asking me to sign papers right now?" Tammy was in disbelief. She had no idea what was happening and why she would need to be signing anything when her husband was lying in a hospital bed. "Someone needs to tell me what's going on," Tammy said, now fuming. She glanced between the attorney and the doctor, who was now already halfway down the hall.

"Tammy," his attorney said, gently nudging her elbow to direct her to a seat, "Are you aware of Joshua's condition?" Tammy remained standing.

"I'm so confused. What condition?" Tammy asked, immediately thinking of everything that could possibly be wrong.

"He has a heart condition called cardiomyopathy," his lawyer said as she began to fill her in on the details of his condition. Everything else she said was a blur. Her legs began to feel like jelly under her and she had to take a seat. Her mother, seeing the concern and heartache in her eyes, rushed to her side to see what was going on.

"What's the matter, baby?"

"I don't know. Why didn't he tell me this? Why is he still playing ball?" she wondered out loud, shaking her head in disbelief.

"As far as I know, he just recently found out. After learning about his condition, he told me that this would be his last season and he was planning to retire, settle down and support you as you pursued your career," his lawyer tried to reassure her.

"Why didn't he tell me this?" Tammy continued to question.

"I'm sure he was going to get around to it. He had me draw up several documents for you last week. I'm sorry that we have to talk about this now."

"Talk about what? I can't talk about anything until I find out how he's doing. Where is the doctor?" she asked, standing and looking around for any person in scrubs and a white coat to return to the waiting area.

"All I know is that the fall was caused by his heart condition. Listen, Tammy. Look at me. I know you're hurting and feeling confused, but we really need to talk about his will and power of attorney."

"Will? I am not going to discuss anything with you right now. I'm sorry, Megan. I know you're doing your job but I can't do this with you right now. I just can't," Tammy said, still looking around for someone who could provide information on Joshua's current condition.

Just as she finished speaking, the doctor returned to the waiting area and called for Tammy. Joshua was now awake and was asking for her. Immediately running to where the doctor was standing, she asked, "Is he awake? Can I see him?"

"Yes, he is asking for you," his doctor said. "Please follow me." Her feet felt like lead as she followed the doctor down the hall, not knowing what she would see or how serious Joshua's condition really was. She said a quick prayer as she arrived in front of his door. The last time she was in the hospital, she had to say good-bye to her grandmother; she was hoping that she didn't have to say good-bye to him too. Taking a deep breath, she entered the hospital room that the doctor led her to.

When she entered the room, he turned his head towards the door, reaching out for her. Running to his side, unable to hold back tears, she asked, "Josh, honey, why didn't you tell me? Are you okay? How are you feeling?" The questions hastily flowed from her lips.

"Honey, slow down. I'm fine. I was planning to tell you about my condition; I just didn't think it was too serious. I'm going to take it easy, though. Don't worry."

"Babe," she said rubbing his hand against her cheek, "you're going to have to reconsider playing ball."

"I know. I am planning to retire this year."

"Do you really think your coach is going to allow you back on that court? Do you really think that I'm going to stand by and watch you hurt yourself? It can't happen. You need to start thinking about early retirement," she said, as encouraging as she could.

"I can't let my team down," he said. He had plans on helping his team win the championship next year.

"Your team will not have you if you continue to go out there," she pleaded with him. "Look at me. I love you and things are starting to go well for us again. I cannot lose you now," Tammy said, as she sat on the bed next to him.

Kissing her hand, he said, "I know. You're right."

"I love you," she said as she heard the door opening. The doctor entered the room to check his vitals. She kissed his cheek and stepped aside so that the doctor could take a look at him. All of a sudden, the heart monitor started beeping frantically. Joshua was having a seizure! She looked back to see his eyes rolling back in his head. "No, no, no, no, no!" she screamed. She rushed back to his side but the doctor grabbed her arms firmly but gently and escorted her outside the door. Nurses were rushing in to help as she stood at the window helpless, watching as they closed the blinds.

"My God! You have to help him. Please!" she said with tears streaming down her face. The familiar smell of the hospital began to bring back memories of her last moments with her grandmother. As she slowly walked back to the waiting area, her mother rushed to her side when she noticed the tears streaming down her face.

"Baby! What's the matter?" her mother asked, fearing the worst.

"Joshua started having a seizure. I don't know what's happening now," she said through sobs.

"Oh baby!" her mother said, hugging her tightly.

"I'm scared, Momma. What am I supposed to do?"

Her mother looked her square in the eye and said, "You are going to be strong and pray for him, that's what you're going to do! It will all be fine. He's going to need you, Tammy. You are going to have to be there for him, because he will need your help to make a full recovery."

"I know, Momma. I know," she said hugging her mother tightly as they walked back to their seats in the waiting room. "Thank you for staying here with me, Momma. Thank you too, Brother," she said squeezing her brother's knee. She was glad that Joshua arranged for them to be there; she had no idea that she would need them right now.

"Well, we are in Boston. You're the only person we know out here. Where else are we going to go?" her brother asked, teasing her in an attempt to lighten the mood. "Don't worry, sis. He's a pretty strong guy. He'll pull through it, especially since he has you waiting on the other side of that room."

"Thanks," she said wiping away her tears. Her brother talked her and their mother into going to the cafeteria to get something to eat while they waited. Tammy sent her mother to bring her something back. She didn't want to miss anything. As they walked away to get some food, she saw Megan again. Fearing the worst, she was finally ready to speak with her about the documents she had mentioned earlier.

CHAPTER 37

∞

Raegan asked Caleb to make a detour before heading out to dinner. She wanted to change into more comfortable clothes since she was still dressed in what she wore to church. When they arrived at her house, she invited him inside to wait on the sofa while she went to change her outfit.

She immediately slid off her blouse and skirt and rummaged through her closet and drawers looking for something comfortable, yet pretty. During her search, she came across one of his old university sleeveless T-shirts that she kept. He used to wear it when he worked out.

She couldn't believe she was still holding on to it after all of this time. That was what she got for not organizing her drawers as planned this past summer. She decided that she would try it on for a quick second just to show him that she still had it in her possession. She slipped on the T-shirt and stood in front of the floor-length mirror to get a glimpse of herself. The hem of the T-shirt hit right above her knees. Excited about the way she looked in the shirt, she danced in the mirror. Her time in the gym paid off, she thought as she flexed in the mirror, showing off her tightened calf muscles and toned legs.

Walking out of the bedroom into the hallway, she peeped around the corner to see what he was doing. He had made himself comfortable and turned on the television. Taking a deep breath, she walked barefoot across the hardwood floor into the living room, dressed in only underwear and his T-shirt.

"I had to get comfortable because it was taking—" Caleb said, stopping mid-sentence when he realized what she was wearing. He immediately took note of her toned legs that seemed to go on for days under the shirt.

"What do you think?" she asked. "Comfortable enough for Chinese food?" she continued as she twirled around in front of him, showing off the T-shirt.

Suddenly, his mouth felt dry. She was absolutely stunning. *She knows what her being dressed like that does to me. Why would she do that? She may have thought it was harmless but it certainly was not.* She just changed his entire mood. Caleb was instantly reminded of sexual encounters they shared in the past. Once they crossed that line when they were together, they always struggled with the issue. They wanted to please God but always found themselves falling short, very short, when it came to sex.

Caleb thought that he had become strong in this area, especially since he had been able to keep his own commitment to celibacy within the last year. In that moment, he figured he must have been fooling himself because all of the sexual feelings he once shared with Raegan came rushing back and he wanted nothing more than to experience that again.

Pulling her onto his lap, he answered her question with a kiss. She hadn't felt a kiss like that in such a long time, ten years to be more precise. Her entire body grew warm with passion and excitement. They both allowed themselves the pleasure of being with one another once again, exploring the passion that bridled deeply inside of them, until they were both satisfied. Finishing off their moments of ecstasy with their mouths caressing each other, Raegan pulled back.

Again, she had broken her vow of celibacy. *But was it so wrong since we really love each other and would likely marry one day?* She rationalized. She now knew that she could not even consider marrying Rico but wasn't so sure how she would deal with the situation.

"It still looks better on you than it does on me," Caleb said as Raegan slid off his lap to stand. He buttoned his shirt and fastened his pants. His heart was still racing from the intimate encounter he just had with her. He hoped she knew that he wasn't after her body but all of her. He wanted her to be his wife and because he had grown spiritually since the last time they were together, that couldn't happen again. He wanted to wait until they married but she needed to understand that he was a man who was visually stimulated. In order to keep his vow of celibacy, they would both have to agree not to have sex until they were married. She would have to agree not to intentionally arouse him.

"Thank you. Compliment well received," she said. "I think I just want to relax and eat pizza now. Is that okay with you?" Raegan asked. She was no longer in the mood to go out. She needed to wrap her head around what just happened. They needed to have a serious conversation to make sure that it didn't happen again.

"Anything you want. I will call to order it in. Anything as long as it isn't supreme pizza, right?" he affirmed.

"Yes. While you do that, I'm going to take a shower and slip into something comfortable, for real this time," she said, picking up her underwear and skipping her way back into her bedroom.

After ordering the pizza, he went to the rental vehicle to pull out one of his bags. He now needed a shower as well and decided that he, too, should get more comfortable. After grabbing his bag, he went back into the house, following the route that Raegan took back into her bedroom.

"Cami, I need a shower as well," he said, speaking over the bathroom fan and shower stream. "Do you have another shower that I can use?"

She directed him to the other bathroom and continued her shower. Just as she was getting dressed, the doorbell rang. *Pizza delivery drivers are fast these days,* she thought.

Caleb had left money on the kitchen counter for the pizza. She paid the delivery driver, gave him a gracious tip and took the pizza to the kitchen table to prepare plates for the two of them. She opened the pizza box and noticed that he had ordered her favorite pizza, meatlovers. When they were together, pepperoni had been her favorite but now she was a huge fan of meatlovers pizza. It looked delicious but she decided that she would wait for him to finish his shower before starting.

Moments later, she watched as he walked through the living room and into the kitchen. She took note of his muscular arms and strong chest. Time had been gracious to him. He was even more handsome than he was years ago. She immediately had to refocus on the food or she was going to find herself in more trouble than she was already in.

"I prepared your plate for you. What do you want to drink?" she asked.

"Do you have any Dr. Pepper by any chance?" he asked.

"No. I have Sprite and lemonade," said Raegan, pushing away from the table, preparing to stand.

"I'll take the Sprite," he said. "I'll get it. You don't have to get up. Is it in the fridge or freezer?"

"Freezer."

"I figured that. I know you like your drinks slushy. Hopefully there's some fizz left in it for me," he said, grabbing the two liter from the freezer and walking to the table to join Raegan.

Caleb blessed the food before they ate a few slices of pizza. During their pizza dinner, Raegan opened the discussion to talk about what just happened.

"Caleb, we need to talk about our lack of control just moments ago," she said, watching his facial expression.

"You're right, Cami. You need to know something. I am practicing celibacy, at least I was until earlier, but I'd like to continue my commitment. I know we struggled with purity in our relationship before, but I know we can do better now. We are much stronger people and should be able to control ourselves."

"I was celibate for two years before my involvement with Rico," Raegan said. She explained the circumstances around her celibacy and her almost marriage to Damian. Raegan was doing well with her commitment to purity until she got involved with Rico. At first she thought she was strong enough to handle the temptation but she was proved wrong. It was much easier to remain celibate when she was not involved in a relationship.

"I can't believe you were almost married, Cami. I have to say that I'm glad that didn't turn out well or else we wouldn't be sitting here right now," he said, reaching for her hand across the table. "We need to pray and repent for having sex and not make that kind of decision again until we make a commitment to one another before God. Can we do that?" Caleb asked. He was certain that she was going to be his wife and he had no problem with waiting for the gift that God would give him in her.

"Sure, I don't want something like this to get in the way of our growth in God and with one another. We need to be able to keep clear heads and hearts," she answered. That was really what she wanted and she was glad that Caleb was on board with that.

They repented for their sin and vowed to remain celibate. Afterwards, they continued eating and table talk. They watched a couple of movies before Caleb retired to his hotel. He couldn't stay over because that would go against the promise they had just made. He kissed her softly on her right cheek and then raised her left hand to his lips and brushed it with a kiss before leaving.

"Let me know when you make it to your hotel and are safely checked in," she said, hugging him tight and resting her head against his chest.

"No doubt," Caleb said, walking to the Jeep rental, unlocking the door with the remote and hopping inside. He winked and waved good-bye as he pulled out of the driveway.

Waving him off, she shut the door and leaned against it for a few minutes. Letting a long sigh flow from her lips, she closed her eyes for a while to remember everything that happened between her and Caleb that day. She always hated to be the one to call off relationships because she didn't like being the bad guy. However, she knew she couldn't worry about that much anymore. She was almost certain there was no future with her and Rico. Now the question became, how would she end things with Rico?

CHAPTER 38

∞

Raegan replayed the events of her weekend with Caleb over and over in her mind. There were moments at work during the week where she mindlessly performed her tasks because her mind wandered off to Caleb and then to Rico and back to Caleb again. She really had no idea what to do now. She needed to talk to someone about her feelings and the facts of each situation, but she was partly ashamed of her behavior.

She had been doing so well with being celibate the past few years, and within the past few months, not only did she break her celibacy but she'd given herself to two guys. What was wrong with her, and what would cause her to act out like that? She was so sure that she was strong enough in her faith to be able to resist such temptations and situations. To prove that she was strong and fixed on not having sex until marriage, she stopped taking birth control pills about two years ago. She felt like there was no need for contraception if she wasn't doing or planning on doing anything that would cause her to get pregnant.

Both she and Kensi made a decision to become celibate around the same time. However, Kensi didn't stop taking her birth control pills. Kensi knew that given the right *or wrong* circumstances, she could possibly find herself needing her pills. Not Raegan. She was certain that she was strong enough and hoped that her actions would encourage Kensi to do the same. After all, they decided they would be each other's accountability partner when it came to premarital sex. They had countless discussions about how to keep themselves out of such situations and what they would do should they find themselves in heated circumstances.

Raegan didn't think about fleeing from temptation this past weekend and, if she was honest with herself, she didn't want to get out of the situation at that time. She wanted to be with Caleb again.

It was time that she had some serious discussions with God. She definitely needed to repent and pray. She needed much strength at this time in her life, because although she knew sex before marriage was wrong, she wanted it and she wanted it very badly. She even dreamed about it last night. She needed to talk with her accountability partner so that she could be encouraged.

She also needed to talk with Rico. She had no idea what she would say to him about all of this, or even if she would mention Caleb at all. It was about time that she faced the reality of the situation with Rico anyway. They could not work. Since she'd opened herself up to him, she felt like she needed to at least try, but with Caleb back in the picture, she didn't really want to. Part of her felt like she needed to work things out with Rico because she had slept with him. If she were to marry him, then maybe breaking her celibacy wouldn't be so bad because she was having sex with her future husband, right? But what would that mean for the time she recently shared with Caleb? If she were to marry him, would the indiscretion with Caleb *fix* the situation with Rico? Her thoughts continued to jump all over the place as she tried to work out a solution.

She needed to talk to Caleb as well. As much as she loved him, he needed to know she couldn't possibly have a future with him until she settled this thing with Rico. She just hadn't quite figured out how she would do that yet. Her phone beeped. She had a text message from Rico that said, *"I need to see you today. It's urgent. Please make time. Thanks."*

Well that didn't sound comforting, she thought. Anytime someone *needed* to see you or talk to you, it was never anything good. She replied and told him that she would meet him during her lunch break. After that exchange, she wasn't able to be as productive as she needed to be. It was hard to focus on work after someone said something like that to her. Simple words but often loaded with some sort of bad news or disappointment.

Raegan spent the rest of the day on conference calls and live meetings. When she wasn't meeting with someone, she was glued to her desk trying to catch up on the work that seemed to keep piling up. She had tons of things to review, because of her transition into her new role, in addition to all of her regular duties. Even with all of that, she still needed to prepare for a presentation that she had to give later in the week.

Rico's message was bothering her and she hoped that she would be able to get away during lunch time to meet him, but she had to cancel and settle for grabbing something quick.

While standing in line at the deli downstairs, the knots in her stomach immediately returned when she heard a familiar voice call her name.

CHAPTER 39

∞

Tammy sat in the waiting room for what seemed like an eternity. Her mind replayed all of the possible outcomes of the situation with Joshua over and over again. She prayed that all would be well, seeing that they missed the last nine years with each other because of her selfishness.

The doctor came over and touched Tammy's shoulder. Her head shot up and she jumped out of her seat, anxiously waiting to hear what the doctor would say.

"Mrs. Archer, everything is just fine," he smiled. That comforted her because that was the first smile coming from him all evening. She then breathed a sigh of relief.

"Thank God! Can I see him?" she asked.

"You can see him in just a moment, but I want to discuss his condition with you. You will be the one caring for him, right?" the doctor asked, wanting to be sure that he was giving care instructions to the right person.

"Yes," she said.

The doctor asked Tammy to follow him into his office. He discussed cardiomyopathy and what that meant for Joshua. He showed her brochures on the condition and told her that it is generally a manageable condition. She had no need to worry about Joshua, although he would have to take it easy for a while.

The doctor reviewed the recovery instructions with Tammy to make sure that she understood the type of care Joshua would need. He really needed to rest and she knew he wouldn't do that if he stayed in Boston. They would have to arrange for him to return to Texas with her when the doctor released him.

"He is definitely going to need you." The doctor reminded her as he stood to escort her out of his office. "I'm going to take you to see him now."

Relieved that all turned out well and that she would get the chance to reconcile with her husband, she happily followed the doctor to Joshua's room.

Running to his side, she immediately planted a kiss on his lips. She was well aware that she should no longer take her time with him for granted. "I'm so glad you're okay," Tammy said after she broke the kiss. She remained close as she cupped the back of his head in her hands.

"Me too. I told you not to worry. Everything is going to be fine," he said, rubbing his hands through her hair and caressing the side of her face.

"While that is true, some changes will have to be made," she said. Tammy pulled away to sit beside him on the bed. She then questioned the doctor about whether or not it was a good idea for him to fly. There was no way she was leaving him in Boston. She still needed to work, and the best thing for both of them was for him to spend some time in Texas.

"I think that's a great idea for his recovery. A change of scenery is always good," the doctor stated and smiled at the two of them. He always felt a sense of satisfaction when his patients were doing well and had loved ones to care for them.

Joshua had to stay in the hospital a couple more days for observation and was free to travel to Texas once the doctor released him.

When the doctor finished checking on him and left the room, Joshua said, "Thank you for staying by my side."

Tammy was a little saddened that he would even think that she would leave him. Although they hadn't been together, she didn't wish him any harm. She still loved him and there was no way she would leave him at a time like this.

"You don't have to thank me. I'm your wife; I wouldn't have it any other way," she said and kissed him once more.

He raised her hand to his lips and gently kissed it. When he proposed, he had no idea that he'd be on his way to Texas. But now that they were reconciling, he didn't care where they lived, as long as they were together.

CHAPTER 40

∞

Raegan was not expecting to see Rico at the sandwich shop since she had to cancel their meeting because of work demands. While standing in line, about to place her order for a meatball marinara sandwich, she heard someone call her name. Immediately recognizing the voice, her stomach twisted into knots and her heart beat rapidly. To her, the beating was so loud, it sounded as if drums were playing in her ears matching the rhythm of her heart.

She slowly turned around and saw Rico walking towards her.

"Hey Raegan, I thought that was you standing in line. How are you?" he asked, seeming a little distant she noticed. He didn't move to embrace her in a hug or offer a kiss on the cheek as usual. He was definitely not behaving the way he normally did, and that made her even more nervous.

"I'm doing well. I've just been very busy today. What are you doing so far away from your office this late in the afternoon?" She thought that it was quite odd because she had never known him to be in that area this late.

"I was just taking a little break. I needed to get some fresh air. I was passing through to go to Starbucks when I happened to glance this way and caught a glimpse of you. Do you have a few minutes to talk?" he asked. He remained standing a few feet away from her, not once showing any ounce of affection. He figured that now was as good a time as any to put his plan into action.

"Well, I was actually going to grab a sandwich and head back upstairs to finish a few things so that I could catch up with you after work. But I guess since we're both here, I have a couple of minutes to spare," she said, stepping out of line, becoming even more uneasy than before. It was a good thing that she wore flats today, because she probably would have toppled over in four-inch heels being as nervous as she was.

"Good. Did you want to order your food first," Rico asked her, nodding toward the short line of customers.

"No, it can wait. I'll be fine. What's up?" she asked, running her hands down the side of her peplum top and skirt as if to smooth out any wrinkles. It was something she did to help ease her anxiety. He motioned for her to follow him as he walked outside of the restaurant. They walked down the hall and took a seat on a wooden bench. Raegan sat down and quietly waited for him to speak.

Taking a deep breath, he found the words to say everything that he'd rehearsed a hundred times to himself that morning on the way to work. Coming up with hundreds of reasons why they wouldn't work out, he settled on something that he thought would certainly be a deal breaker and would flip the tables to get her to break up with him. "Let me first start by saying that I'm sorry and I had no idea," he said.

Her stomach twisted in a way that she never knew it could as she held her breath. This could not be good. *Okay, just breathe,* she thought. *You don't know what he's going to say, just relax and listen.* "Okay," she mustered. "Just go on."

"A couple of days ago, I received a phone call from an ex-girlfriend. Well, she wasn't really a girlfriend, but someone who I used to sleep with. She said that she has been diagnosed with genital herpes and that I could be infected as well. And let me just say that I have never had any outbreaks or any signs that I could possibly be infected."

Oh no! she thought. *What in the world is happening? How could this be happening to me? Oh, Lord, what about Caleb. I just had sex with him.* For a few seconds, she didn't hear anything else he was saying. *What about my future? This is going to ruin me! Okay, breathe. Go get tested, Raegan.*

"Are you serious?" she asked, hoping that he would tell her that it was all a lie and that he just wanted to break up with her. "Please tell me this isn't true. How long have you known about this?" Her breathing became labored as she started getting angry.

"Yes, Raegan, I'm serious and I just told you that I found out a few days ago," Rico said calmly as he continued with his manufactured story.

"Why would you wait to tell me? Don't you think you should have mentioned this to me as soon as it was mentioned to you?" She asked, becoming furious.

"I wanted to get tested first."

"And?"

"And what?"

"What were the results?" She asked. She couldn't believe him. If she weren't near her workplace, she would have slapped him.

"They were negative, but you still should get tested," he advised calmly.

"Don't worry. I will," she said, her voice hard and eyes cold.

"You're actually taking this a lot better than I thought you would. I figured you would be trying to kill me when I told you that," He said. He sat hunched over on the bench with his head low, no longer looking at her.

"Are you sure that this was some old fling and not someone you recently had sex with?" she asked through clenched teeth, wondering if he had been unfaithful to her just as she had been unfaithful to him.

"Are you trying to say that I'm cheating on you?" he asked incredulously. He was getting too caught up in the moment. He wasn't cheating on her; he was cheating on his wife with her, but she didn't need to know that.

"You are so ridiculous. Don't try to turn this thing around on me when you're sitting beside me, practically telling me that you may have given me an incurable disease! Bye Rico! Please don't worry about trying to call me again," she spat as she stood up to walk away.

"Raegan, wait. I'm not done," he said grabbing her arm.

"Oh yes, you are!" she said as she snatched her arm away from him, trying not to cause a scene. People were already starting to stare.

"Raegan, we should cool things down a bit, don't you think? All of this just has me thinking about how I can't be the man you need me to be."

"That's the best thing that came out of your ungrateful mouth this afternoon. Good-bye!" she said, walking away without giving him a second glance. "Bastard!" She said under her breath as she stormed away.

Her previous nervousness had now turned into bitterness. She was bitter, angry and feeling pretty malicious. She really wanted to hurt him, but now she had to think about herself and explain this foolishness to Caleb. Her anger immediately changed to guilt. It was her fault. She seduced Caleb, and now look at the price that they both potentially would have to pay. This entire situation just seemed to keep getting worse and worse. There was no way that she could stay at work now; she had to get to the doctor's office. It was only 2 p.m. so hopefully her doctor had an opening. She walked as quickly as possible back to the elevator bank. On the way, she pulled out her cell to call the doctor's office.

"Good afternoon, thanks for calling Dr. Johnson and Dr. Mallory's nurses' station. How may I help you?"

"Good afternoon, this is Raegan Sanders. Is there any chance that Dr. Mallory can see me today?"

"You called at the perfect time. Dr. Mallory just had a cancellation. If you can get here by 3:00, she can see you then." The nurse said. She then took the details of Raegan's reason for needing an appointment and added Raegan to Dr. Mallory's patient schedule for the 3:00 time slot.

"Excellent! Thank you. I'm on my way," she said, entering the elevator. When she arrived at her floor, she quickly entered the double paneled glass doors and walked as fast as she could, without running, to her office. She sent an e-mail to her manager, letting her know that she was taking sick leave for the rest of the day, threw her things into her brown leather Coach briefcase, snapped it closed and raced back out of her office, without closing the door or turning off the light, and headed back to the elevators.

As she waited for the elevators, she began to think the worst of everything. She lost Rico but she was actually glad about that. In fact, it was sort of a relief to be free of him, but obviously freedom didn't come without a price. If she was infected, she felt like he would somehow be a part of her forever. Ugh! She couldn't imagine the thought. *What if I were to lose Caleb with all of this too? Maybe he would understand. Maybe I wouldn't have to mention it if my test results came back negative.* She had to pull herself together and make it past this first.

The elevator finally arrived after what seemed like at least fifteen minutes. She glanced at her watch to see that it had only been two minutes, but with everything that was going on in her life right now, it seemed like forever. She stepped into the elevator, pressed the ground floor button and checked her face in the mirrored panels. She hoped that she didn't look as disheveled as she felt. Smoothing her curls and her clothes, she did a quick eye, nose and teeth check right as the elevator arrived at the ground floor. As soon as the doors opened, she walked as fast as she could without looking like someone was chasing her or like she was picking up pace in a marathon.

When she finally made it to her coupe, she opened the door, slung the briefcase into the passenger seat, slid into the car, buckled up, ignited the engine and sped through the parking garage. She knew that was dangerous in more ways than one, but she was a woman on a mission. Exiting the garage, she maneuvered her way through traffic on the verge of speeding to arrive at the doctor's office at 2:55 p.m. She left her car with valet, grabbed a ticket stub and rushed into the building.

Raegan prayed and asked God to help her through this. She couldn't believe how drastically her life changed over the last few months. She vowed not to have sex again until she got married, not even with Caleb, no matter how great the sex was. She had to get her life back in order. She felt like she was so far out of line with God that she couldn't feel His presence. She knew He was there but it just felt like there was so much in between her and her heavenly Father. She promised herself that she would work to get back on track and that she would be honest with her accountability partner. After all, it didn't do her any good having an accountability partner if she wasn't allowing her to hold her accountable.

CHAPTER 41

∞

Raegan finally made it home after weaving through the rush hour traffic. She called Kensi to have a serious discussion with her while she made dinner. Hopefully Kensi was home from work or at least some place where she could talk. After deciding on tilapia and fresh steamed veggies, she placed the fish in the sink filled with cold water, picked up her cell phone, and dialed Kensi's number. It was time to come clean.

"Hello," Kensi answered merrily. She was in a great mood.

"Hey girl! How are you?"

"I'm great Rae. What's going on?"

"Way too much. Can you talk?" Raegan asked hopefully.

"Sure can. I worked from home today because I'm preparing to go out of town again for work on tomorrow. They are sending me to Palm Springs, California, for training. I am looking forward to it. Anything at this point to get away from these freezing temperatures in New York. What's up with you, though?" she asked, sorting through her laundry to prepare for her trip.

"Are you sitting down? If not, you probably should," Raegan said. Raegan felt drained just thinking about everything going on in her life. She figured Kensi would feel emotionally drained as well after she poured her heart out. She really just wanted to take a nap, but she needed to eat something and wrap up some unfinished work.

"Okay. You don't sound like your usual chipper self. Tell me what's wrong. Did Rico or Caleb do something crazy? Do I need to come out there and straighten someone out for you, girl? I can make a detour on my way to Cali if you need me to," Kensi said, trying to cheer up her friend.

"You may need to straighten me out as well." Raegan paused to collect her thoughts. She knew that her friend wouldn't judge her, but she couldn't help but judge herself. It felt like her life was spiraling out of control. "I slept with Rico, Kensi." She paused again waiting for Kensi to respond, but her confession was greeted by silence.

Leaning forward with her elbows on the kitchen table and her head resting in the palm of her hands, Raegan continued. "I know it's insane. I've gone through it over and over again and I can't believe that I broke my celibacy so easily. I guess I thought that he was the one and that ultimately it wouldn't matter too much if we had sex before we got married, because we were in fact getting married. Or so I thought."

"Raegan, we both know that there aren't any guarantees when it comes to things like that. I wish you would have come to me and at least had given me the chance to talk you out of it."

"That's just the thing Kens. It's not like I contemplated it. I got caught up in the moment several times. Once after telling myself I wouldn't do it again, I allowed him to sleep over. I woke up the next morning with his head in between my legs. It was hard to stop things after that. At that point, I wanted it. I was such a fool." Rambling on, Raegan said, "You know I think I'm more upset with myself for putting myself in that kind of predicament and allowing things to go too far. I mean, I know better. I don't know what happened to me."

"We all get weak, Raegan. You, my friend, just got caught up. It happens to all of us at some point, whether it's with sex or some other sin that we're dealing with."

"I suppose I had a temporary lapse in judgment. I sometimes feel like this celibacy thing and trying to do things God's way when it comes to relationships is just too hard and I will possibly end up alone, you know?"

"Now Raegan, cut that silly talk out. You and I both know and believe that the right guy for you wouldn't mind waiting and that he should be on the same path spiritually anyway."

Raegan knew that Kensi's words rang true. She now believed that she and Caleb were getting on track and focused on doing things the right way. She was a bit more encouraged since they'd been having many talks lately about what they want in life both spiritually and with each other. Both Raegan and Caleb desired to please God in all of their ways and didn't want their relationship to get in the way of that.

Kensi continued interrupting Raegan's thoughts. "Well, I can tell you right now that part of your problem is that you're focused on the wrong thing. What happened to cause you to shift your focus from God's timing to your timing?" Kensi knew that Raegan could get ahead of herself because she deeply desired to be married. Raegan's relationship with Damian was proof of that.

Letting out a long sigh, Raegan finally said, "I don't know. I wish I knew. But hold on, there's a whole lot more to this story."

"I'm all ears," Kensi said as she zipped her suitcase. She plopped down on the bed, stretched out on her stomach, kicked her heels in the air and waited for Raegan to continue.

"Caleb and I have been talking a lot more and spending time together when he comes to town working on his transition to the area. In fact, I recently slept with him, too." Raegan paused. She knew there wouldn't be silence on the line after she dropped that bomb.

"Oh my goodness Raegan! All of sudden, you're like some kind of sex kitten or something? What's going on with you? As your friend and accountability partner, I need you to cease all of those shenanigans. No more of that."

"Shenanigans?" Raegan asked laughing.

"Yeah, girl. You are out of control. We're supposed to be helping each other through this celibacy thing, but you've completely cut me out of it. I must admit that I'm disappointed in you. This is so out of character for you."

"I know. I have resolved not to have sex again until marriage. Sex with both of them has clouded my judgment, leaving me so confused, at least until today," Raegan said as she told Kensi about Rico's confession of possibly having transmitted an STD to her.

"Raegan, I'm so sorry honey. Talking about a consequence?! I really hope things turn out well and that your test is negative."

"Yeah…me too. I'm praying it's negative…" From the moment Rico gave Raegan the news, she had been pleading with God to have mercy on her for her lapses in judgment. The weight of everything was becoming too much for her and she wasn't prepared to deal with any of it.

"You know Raegan, oftentimes, that's how we are as God's children. We forget about Him and get ourselves tangled up in mess and then want Him to fix it. Most of the time we know the right thing to do but we choose the selfish route, only thinking about ourselves, and seek to fulfill the pleasure of our flesh," Kensi reminded Raegan.

"I know. I've made a long string of wrong choices over the past few weeks. Thankfully God is a forgiving God!" Raegan was reminded of the scriptures that she was holding close to her heart: Psalm 103:8-12

The Lord is compassionate and gracious, slow to anger, abounding in love. He will not always accuse, nor will he harbor his anger forever; he does not treat us as our sins deserve or repay us according to our iniquities. For as high as the heavens are above the earth, so great is his love for those who fear him; as far as the east is from the west, so far has he removed our transgressions from us.

"Wait!" Kensi said as if a light bulb had gone off in her head. "Raegan, have you told Caleb?!?"

"Not yet. I'm waiting until I receive my test results."

"Eww. Are you sure that you should wait to tell him? I mean, that is pretty serious business."

"I know it is, but I need to know what my results are before I mention it to him, I think." Raegan already felt guilty about everything because she was the one who initiated sex with Caleb. She hoped that if her results were negative that he wouldn't take it so hard. Raegan also felt like Rico deceived her, so she was having an issue getting past that. "And you know what? Something just doesn't feel right with Rico's story, but I don' know if I should even be concerned with it anymore," she told Kensi.

"This is all pretty heavy Raegan. I just wish we would have had the chance to talk before all of this happened."

"I know. I'm sorry. I guess an even bigger part of me wanted to go through with it, and that is why I didn't call you. Of course, I knew you were going to talk me out of it and that wasn't what I wanted. It's almost like Coca-Cola to me. You know I don't drink soda but every now and again, maybe once a year, I will have a taste of it. I am reminded of how good it is, although I know it isn't good for me. The taste is so satisfying that I have to have that Coca-Cola again the next day and possibly the day after that, until I get my fill of it. It's not until three days later that I realized I have done my body a disservice, cheated on my diet and practically went crazy by going overboard drinking so much of it in such a short period of time," Raegan said, trying to explain why she kept making the same choice over and over again. She slouched down in the breakfast nook, sulking over her mistakes.

"Really Raegan? Coca-Cola?" she asked laughing out loud. "You are too funny but I think I understand. There is something in that drink that's addictive, and sex can certainly be addictive as well. I'm pretty sure that God knows that and that is why God intended for it to be preserved for married couples."

"I agree," Raegan said. And she really did agree, but while caught up in the moment, her choices proved otherwise.

"Raegan, you know you can call me anytime, especially if you're feeling weak and need someone to remind you that you can make it and that God has created you for a higher purpose. Next time, remember that those few minutes of carnal pleasure are not worth God's eternal blessings. I believe in you Rae. You've done well for so long. God is a forgiving God. Just remember to release it all to Him."

"Thanks friend. I'm sending you an air hug right now. Thanks for helping me feel better about myself and this entire situation. I have gotten myself into a big mess here," Raegan said.

"You're welcome. You'll get through it. I know you will. God has so much more in store for you," Kensi encouraged her friend. She knew that Raegan needed her. After hanging up the phone, she silently vowed to be a little more probing in order to do her part as Raegan's accountability partner.

CHAPTER 42

∞

Trying to gain her composure as much as possible before answering Caleb's call, Raegan shut her eyes tight, let out a long, deep breath and pressed *answer*. "Hey!" she said in the cheeriest voice she could. The possibility of having contracted an STD weighed heavily on her. The idea that she may have passed it on to him and the fact that she was withholding that information made her feel even more guilty.

"Hello beautiful. You were on my mind so I was just calling to check on you. I am on my way to a going-away happy hour in my honor, but wanted to take a few seconds to hear your beautiful voice."

Having mixed emotions about the fact that the call was going to be short, she answered, "I'm okay. I am about to eat dinner and then I have to get to work. I have a ton of work to get done; I didn't get a lot accomplished in the office today."

"Why is that?" he asked. His concern was evident in his voice. "Is everything okay?"

"Yes, it will be. I just have a ton of work piling up with the transition into my new role," she said, telling a half-truth. She could handle work and didn't care about how much she would have to take on; what she couldn't handle was being marked with a sexually transmitted disease for the rest of her life, especially from someone she no longer had a desire to be with. Her stomach turned just thinking about it.

"I have total confidence in you; you are one of the strongest and most efficient women I know." He asked, "What are you having for dinner?"

"Baked fish and steamed veggies."

"Umm, that sounds good and healthy. Will you promise to prepare me some of that when I settle into town?"

"If you still want it by then, most certainly," she said, not referring to the time but to what she had to share with him. In no way could she share it over the phone, she decided; it would just have to wait until he returned.

"Of course I will. One last thing I want to share with you before you go. I am certain that this will cheer you up."

"All right! Let's hear it," she said as she prepared her plate.

"We got the house—the very first house we toured!! The realtor called me a couple of hours ago," he said, grinning. Things were starting to come together for them. He was one step closer to getting the life he wanted with her.

"Oh my gosh! Really?! That is so exciting!" she said. That news really did lift her spirits but she knew that it wasn't her house and would probably never be when he heard what she had to tell him.

"Yeah, it definitely is. Looks like we have another reason to celebrate," he said, thinking of their upcoming celebration of her promotion.

"Thank you for sharing the news. That definitely brightened my day a little…"

"Then I've done my duty for the evening…I will let you eat and get to work. I just made it to the happy hour. And Cami…remember that you don't have to worry. Everything will turn out well; pace yourself and try not to stress," said Caleb, trying to encourage her.

"Okay, thanks. I will do that. Have a good night," Raegan said softly.

"Good night, beautiful," said Caleb as he ended the call. The sound of her voice always excited him and he hoped that would never change. As for Raegan, just the sound of his deep tenor voice had her heart flipping and pulse racing. The butterflies that she needed. She was glad that he called because she felt somewhat comforted, for the time being, in the midst of this thunderstorm that she was experiencing.

***

One week had gone by since Raegan's doctor's appointment. She worked to keep herself busy so that she wouldn't worry about her test results. She had no idea how to handle a situation like this and she was scared out of her mind. *Bastard!* she thought to herself, but truly she couldn't put all of the blame on him; she got herself into this mess.

The doctor's office called to set an appointment so that she could come in and talk about her test results. *This could not be good*, she thought. She was sure that the doctor said that they would give her the results over the phone. The earliest they could see her was tomorrow morning. She was going to go crazy until then. There was no way she could sit at work and actually be productive with this doctor's appointment looming over her head. She decided to take personal leave for the rest of the day so that she could find something that would occupy her time. The movies! She could get lost in someone else's story. She drove straight to the theater near her house to catch any movie that would take her mind off her own problems.

Back at home later, she was still restless. After pacing for half an hour, she decided to distract herself and channel her restless energy into cleaning. Starting with her dresser, she pulled out the two top drawers and dumped the contents on her bed. Sorting through her underwear, she found old love letters and greeting cards from ex-boyfriends. She paused to read a few cards and letters. Most of the cards brought a smile to her face as she remembered old loves.

"I think I've done all right with the guys I've dated," she spoke to herself. "Most of them were pretty good guys, so I don't know how I allowed myself to get tangled up with this nut," she said, opening a letter from Rico that she had printed from her computer. The letter read:

Well for all of my 32 years I have always had hesitations when it came to women. My natural analytical ability allows me to see thoughts before words are ever spoken and due to that I have typically stayed away from giving my heart to unworthy women.

As I search this world looking for the woman GOD created just for me, I often have asked myself are the standards I have set here too much? Is there a woman out there that can actually live up to what I want? Hmmmm... Women of the past have only measured up to about 50% of what I want, and that's no offense to any woman I have dated. I look for a woman who has a relationship with GOD, who is striving to be a better person, intelligent, gorgeous, family-oriented, strong, compassionate, with a heart willing to give and a mind willing to accept. Now these things may sound simple, but believe me to find these things in one person have been impossible.

And then you appeared! You have everything I desire, everything I prayed for, everything I need, but the funny thing about requiring people to meet a certain standard, we as people must be able to handle exactly what we are asking for. And I openly admit I was not, you are so perfect that it scared me. I started to doubt myself, to doubt our relationship, to tell myself I wasn't ready to LOVE, but as hard as I attempt to come off, as many excuses as I tried to make, to no avail. My heart and mind were torn, my heart desires you, but my mind tried to cause me to lean toward some "standard" of time. But who cares about time, and GOD's time is not our own, if I asked GOD to heal my body would I not expect an immediate recovery, so why is it that when I asked GOD to place my wife in my path do I now try to push her away. So I apologize for ever doubting you or us, for not recognizing your worth and for every moment that I caused your heart to be weary. I thank GOD for you, I thank you for your time, your passion, your advice, your compromise, your mind, and your heart.

All of my life I have kept my heart hidden as a measure of protection, but on this day I present you with my heart. I recently told a group of people that relationships were in my mind Algebra, I myself being the constant and the woman being the variable, but on this day I stand corrected, every theory I have regarding relationships you have canceled, every doubt you have reassured me. Thank you for taking a risk on me, for being a real WOMAN, for the kisses, hugs, dinners, time, and even the soap operas that you force me to watch (smile).

Raegan Sanders, with this note, I confess to you that I will be not only a better man, but the best man I can be. I confess that I will always communicate with you, always be faithful and keep our best interest in mind at all times. I confess that YOU ARE THE BEST THING THAT HAS EVER HAPPENED TO ME. Again I recognize and appreciate you as a woman, I recognize you as my queen, and I will always cherish you and treat you as such.

You are respected and you are loved.

I am Rico and this is my confession.

"Wow. And this is the same guy who thought I was trying to pressure him into marriage. Dude is either a great writer or a great liar. Maybe a combination of both? There has to be something more to him. I can just feel it," she said, tossing the letter to the trash.

The mere thought of everything that Rico was putting her through when he was no longer in the picture made her physically ill. At that moment, all of her movie snacks made their way back up – from the popcorn to the fruit gummy candy. "Ugh! I despise you!" she screamed at the letter in the trash as she pulled herself up from the toilet.

CHAPTER 43

∞

Raegan needed to confirm her suspicions regarding Rico so she Googled him once more. Many results came up when she searched his name. The more she searched and clicked each link that seemed like it would provide new information, the warmer the back of her neck became. Bit by bit, each link seemed to provide a little more information about Rico's secret life.

She finally came across a link to a fundraising gala sponsored by some association of nurses. She wasn't sure why that particular link would show up in the search; he wasn't a nurse. She was about to scroll right past it because she thought that it was irrelevant to the kind of information she was searching for, but decided to check it out anyway.

Clicking on the link, she scrolled down the page, not really noting anything. As she was about to exit the page, she caught a glimpse of his name, highlighted from her search. There it was as plain as the sun shining in the summer in Texas, a photo of Rico and his wife, Chloe, dated within the last month. The caption under the picture mentioned something about his wife being an outstanding nurse and being honored at the gala for her contributions to the organization and the hospital. Suddenly feeling physically ill, she ran into the restroom and threw up again.

Raegan washed the beads of sweat from her forehead and gurgled mouthwash. She couldn't believe that the same man who wrote the letter she'd just read was the same married man standing in that picture. *How in the world was he able to pull this off?*

"I swear I'm going to kill him!" she screamed with rage. Now she felt like an even bigger fool. Someone else's husband. "Lord, please forgive me. I didn't know. I would have never even given him any attention had I known. I guess this explains the cheap dates, the calls at work during the day, the text messages in the evenings, the money going to his mom, never visiting his apartment, his attitude when I wanted to discuss his financial situation. I've slept with a total stranger!" She continued ranting as she clicked through the pictures.

"Why would he lie to me and lead me on the way he did? To such a great extent? Was the sex even that important? He has to be insane!" she continued to rant, wondering how she should handle the situation. *Should I tell his wife? Should I stay out of it? Even after all that I've done, I didn't and wouldn't go this low. Compared to this craziness, spending time with Caleb while still in a relationship with Rico wasn't all that bad.*

"I guess while I'm at it, maybe I need to Google Caleb as well. You can never be too sure these days," she said, intent on putting her investigative skills to work. She even put in a few phone calls to old classmates in an attempt to squeeze information out of them about Caleb. Many of the articles she found about him were related to work, with the exception of his social media accounts. *Looks like he has been very successful as an architect. He didn't make it sound as if it was such a big deal, but these articles give the impression that he is highly regarded in his industry, not only in Georgia but across the U.S. He should have drawn up the designs for his home instead of buying someone else's home,* she thought.

Satisfied that she didn't find any terrible skeletons in Caleb's closet, she closed her laptop and returned to her task. Staring at the heap of clothes on her bed, she decided to put them back into the drawers as they were before. She was in no mood to organize anything. In fact, she was mentally drained. She took a shower, climbed into bed and tried to work through her issues in her sleep.

CHAPTER 44

∞

Raegan spent the drive to her doctor's appointment praying and asking God for forgiveness and a fresh start. She asked that God show her mercy during this time and to give her peace regardless of her test results. She wanted to be close to Him again and live in a way that brought Him glory. She realized that she had drifted so far away from Him in the past couple of months, in hopes of becoming a wife, that she gained an enormous amount of heartache. She prayed:

My Lord, my God! I know that I've been completely outside of Your will lately and I ask Your forgiveness. Forgive me for breaking my celibacy vow to You. Forgive me for acting as if I wanted to be married more than I wanted a relationship with You. Right now, I ask that You show me mercy. Have mercy on me Lord when I go into this doctor's office. I have recommitted myself to You already but I want You to know that I choose Your way and not my own. I will trust in You to help me through this. Thank You for being slow to anger and abounding in love. Thank You for Your love and compassion and for not treating me as my sins deserve. Thank You for loving me even in this. In Jesus' name, Amen.

In the midst of her prayers, she was reminded of God's faithfulness through a song that came on the radio. "Thank You Lord," she breathed. "I can do this with You by my side," said Raegan as she joined the artist in song, pulling up to the doctor's office.

Giving her keys to valet, she stepped out of the car, only to be met by the wind whipping her across the face. She quickly reached back into the car to grab her peacoat. *The cowl-neck sweater is not enough today*, she thought. As she walked through the revolving doors, her stomach began to churn in knots once again. "You are going to be all right girl, no matter what happens," she said in an effort to encourage herself. When she arrived at the elevator bank, her knees buckled slightly. She didn't know if it was because of her boots or the anxiety. Pressing the button, she noticed that her hands were even a little shaky. "Girl, you have got to calm down," she whispered to herself. She didn't want anyone to think that she belonged in another doctor's office for standing alone talking to herself.

Exiting the elevators and walking to the front desk to sign in, she felt as if she was walking into doom. She knew that things would be all right but that still didn't help her nerves, especially since the doctor *needed* to see her. As soon as she checked in and walked to the back, the nurse opened the door to the waiting area and called her name. She didn't get a chance to sit down.

"Good morning Raegan," the nurse said and smiled. "You're our first patient today. Come on back." Handing a plastic cup to Raegan, the nurse said, "I'll need a urine sample. When you're done, meet me in room 11."

Raegan did as the nurse instructed and went into room 11 to wait for Dr. Mallory. As soon as she sat down, Dr. Mallory came into the room. *They are moving quickly this morning*, she thought. She had taken the entire day off work because she didn't know what to expect today.

"Good morning Raegan. How have you been? I hope you haven't been stressing out over your test results," said Dr. Mallory peering over glasses looking at Raegan, while holding her medical file up to her chest. Taking a seat, she explained Raegan's results.

"Raegan, we tested you for everything and all the results were negative." She paused, waiting for Raegan to breathe a sigh of relief. "Now you can relax," the doctor said and smiled.

"Thank you Lord!" Raegan said smiling. A huge weight was lifted off her shoulders. "I was so worried. This is such a relief!"

Smiling at Raegan's expression of gratitude, the doctor continued. "Raegan, your bloodwork showed some interesting results. It looks like you may be pregnant. Just to confirm, we're going to perform a vaginal ultrasound this morning. I'm going to leave for a few minutes. Undress from the waist down, cover up with one of the paper sheets here and sit on the table for me. I'll be back in a few minutes."

Raegan's hands, knees and feet were shaking. *Pregnant.* If someone saw her, they would have thought that it was because of the cold doctor's office but Raegan knew better. She was scared out of her mind! What would she do with a baby? *Oh, Lord! Whose baby is it? Please Lord don't let it be Rico's.* She'd been so caught up in everything going on that she didn't realize she missed her period. "I need a calendar," she said, searching the doctor's office for a calendar. "My phone! Duh!" she said rambling through her purse to look at the phone calendar, trying to reconcile the dates.

She couldn't be that far along because she did have her period last month and she was now only a week late. She hadn't slept with Rico since she had her last period, so that brought some sort of relief to her. But then again, that all depended on how far along she was. She often heard about women having periods while they were pregnant. Maybe she was one of them. She undressed, covered herself in the sheet and lay down on the table covering her face with her arm. Once again, she prayed. If anyone knew how she was feeling and could get her though it, it was

God. Interrupted by the opening of the door, she jerked up into a sitting position.

"Raegan dear, you can lie back down. You will need to be lying down for the ultrasound," said Dr. Mallory. Covering the long stick-like object with a condom, the doctor rubbed some sort of gel on it and inserted it into Raegan to get a closer view of what was going on in her uterus. The doctor sat quietly, observing the object on the screen, while Raegan observed her. She tried her best to read the doctor's facial expression but that didn't help. Turning the monitor to Raegan, Dr. Mallory explained the sonogram results.

"Raegan, you are definitely pregnant. Based on the measurements here, you are about 6 and 1/2 weeks along. I know this is shocking news for you, so take some time and let me know what you want to do about this pregnancy," her doctor said, printing a picture and removing the object from Raegan's body. She reached her hand out to Raegan to help her sit up.

"I don't need any time to think about it. I'm going to have this baby," Raegan said. She was mortified at the thought of any other option. In Raegan's mind, having the baby *was* the only option. She was still in shock but now also in love with what appeared to be a peanut on the ultrasound photo. She was scared out of her mind and had no idea how to be a mother, but she would give the little baby the very best of her.

"Great!" Her doctor smiled. "Congratulations! Make an appointment to return to my office in about six weeks. We're going to be seeing a lot of each other over the next nine months. Get some rest and try not to stress. You have a little person growing inside of you to think about now," she said, hugging Raegan. "Have a great day!"

Raegan sat on the table in disbelief for what seemed like an eternity, after hearing Dr. Mallory close the door behind her, but only five minutes had passed. She dressed and walked to the nursing station, all the while staring at the sonogram printout in disbelief. *Pregnant.*

The nurse gave her tons of literature on pregnancy along with many packets of prenatal vitamins. "Take one of these each day, after a meal," the nurse said. After several clicks on the computer, the nurse had scheduled her next appointment. "Alrighty, here is an appointment reminder card. We'll see you in six weeks. Congratulations!" the nurse said with a huge grin.

Leaving the doctor's office she was filled with many different emotions. She definitely wasn't expecting the doctor to give her this kind of news. How was she going to tell Caleb? her friends? her mother? The uncertainties kept piling up. She decided that she didn't feel like dealing with any of this today. She stopped to pick up some of her favorite snacks, grabbed a few redbox movies, and went home to relax.

When she made it home, she put her snacks aside until after lunchtime. She was hungry so she scrambled a couple of eggs and prepared grits and toast. Sitting down to eat, she noticed that she had a missed call from Caleb. "Oh yeah, that's right! He is coming to town today. I completely forgot with all of the craziness going on in my life," she said. Checking the voicemail, she noted that was the reason for his call. He was reminding her about his trip to town that day and asked that she meet him at the house around 2:00 p.m. "Sure, I can do that," she said to the voicemail.

"Hey, I just listened to your voicemail," she said to Caleb on the line.

"Great. Can you meet me at two? Didn't you take off work today?"

"Yes, I did."

"Perfect. Are you all right?" Caleb asked. He knew nothing about her doctor's appointment.

"Yep. I just needed some time to myself to relax." She wasn't sure how or when she would share the news with him. She wondered how he would take it.

"Are you sure you're up for stopping by the house?" he asked. He noticed that she sounded different, like something was bothering her.

"Of course. I'll need some fresh air by then anyway."

"Awesome!" Caleb sent her the address and ended the call. He was very much looking forward to seeing her again. He really missed her beautiful smile while back in

Georgia. All of that was about to change now that he would be getting the keys to their new home today.

****

Raegan took special care to touch up her curls, brush her teeth again, wash and cleanse her face and change clothes. Making sure her physical appearance was in order, her mind went to the little person that was growing inside her uterus. She paused her primping to rub her belly. She hadn't decided when she would tell Caleb or how she would share everything that went on with her over the past couple of weeks. She wasn't even sure how he would feel about the baby. Although he mentioned wanting to start a family, she didn't know if he wanted to start so soon and before they were married.

In an effort to drown out her issues, Raegan sang to the top of her lungs on her way to meet Caleb. When she pulled up to his new home, he was standing in the doorway, waiting for her. When he saw her, he came outside to help her out of the car. Opening her door and reaching for her hand, he guided her down the long pathway that they both adored when they first saw the home. He opened the French glass doors and gestured for her to enter first. She was amazed at what she saw. Rose petals and candles adorned the entryway.

She turned around to see Caleb on one knee holding open a blue box.

"Cami, I know that we've only recently reconnected, but I know what I want and that is a life with you. Say you'll grow old in this house with me. Cami, will you be my wife?" he asked.

Raegan was absolutely stunned. Although she just asked God for a fresh start, she didn't know that this was the kind of start that she was going to get. She wanted to say yes. She believed that they could work out whatever differences that they might have. However, she didn't want to rush things and end up in a tumultuous situation, much like the one she currently found herself in. And what about the baby? There was much to discuss before she could give any answer. Her thoughts and her heart warred with one another until all she could say was, "I'm pregnant."

Getting out of the kneeling position, Caleb stood up in disbelief. He never imagined that the answer to his proposal would be a confession. He paced back and forth, rubbing his hands through his head. He didn't know whether to be excited or not. He knew that he had inserted himself in sort of a messy situation, being that she was still dating someone else when he came back into her life, but what now?

Moving closer to Caleb, she placed her purse on the kitchen island, removed her coat and grabbed his hand to keep him from pacing.

"Is it our baby?" Caleb asked. He gently rubbed her stomach for a moment and then returned his gaze to hers waiting for an answer.

Raegan wasn't sure how to answer that question because she didn't really know.

"You slept with Rico, right?" Caleb asked, sensing her hesitation.

"Yeah. It was stupid," she said.

"It's over now? Completely over?" He gazed at her with a look that was serious but that carried so much acceptance and love she wondered how she could have ever walked away from this man.

"Yes. It's over. You're the only man I want. If you'll still have me. Well, if you'll have *us*." She looked at her belly, placing his hands there again and covering them with her own.

"I don't care whose baby it is. It's your baby, and that means it's our baby. So, what do you say? Will you marry me?" Caleb loved Raegan and dared not let anything get in between them this time around. He intended to show her that he loved her no matter what.

"Of course I will!" Raegan squealed with a smile so huge, he could practically see all of her teeth. Caleb slid the three carat ring onto her finger and she happily accepted it. She was finally going to have the life she always thought she'd have—with Caleb.

Acknowledgements

To my husband who has supported me throughout my writing journey, I love you dearly. *Forever I do.*

 To my children, Eden and Ethan - Mommy loves you more than words could ever say.

To my parents and sisters- I love you and thank you for always believing in me

To my friends who have taken the time to read and reread my manuscript, giving valuable feedback, I love you. I wish each of you more love, joy and happiness than you ever thought possible!

To my editor Cheryl and Graphic Designer BJ O'Neal – thank you for your part in helping this dream come to life.

To my cousins Vicki & Keisha – Way back when, we swapped romance novels and shared our love for reading. I hope that this is one that you'll enjoy and forever keep in rotation.

To my readers - Thank you for your continued support.

About the Author

Natasha has authored The Life Your Spirit Craves and Not Without You. Through her writing and speaking engagements, she hopes to inspire women to love themselves and reach their maximum potential in Christ. When she isn't writing, she is spending time with her husband and two children. She enjoys cooking (eating) and reading. She is also a huge fan of the shows Covert Affairs, NCIS:LA and The Good Wife. For more information about upcoming projects or events, visit her website: www.natashafrazier.com